DESTINY SECOND TO NONE

SCHOLASTIC INC.

TO MY BROTHER MICHAEL, WHOSE MIDDLE SCHOOL
MACHINATIONS RIVALED DJ'S

If you purchased this book without a cover, you should be aware that this book is stolen property. It was reported as "unsold and destroyed" to the publisher, and neither the author nor the publisher has received any payment for this "stripped book."

Copyright © 2024 by Destiny Howell

All rights reserved. Published by Scholastic Inc., *Publishers since 1920.* SCHOLASTIC and associated logos are trademarks and/or registered trademarks of Scholastic Inc.

The publisher does not have any control over and does not assume any responsibility for author or third-party websites or their content.

No part of this publication may be reproduced, stored in a retrieval system, or transmitted in any form or by any means, electronic, mechanical, photocopying, recording, or otherwise, without written permission of the publisher. For information regarding permission, write to Scholastic Inc., Attention: Permissions Department, 557 Broadway, New York, NY 10012.

This book is a work of fiction. Names, characters, places, and incidents are either the product of the author's imagination or are used fictitiously, and any resemblance to actual persons, living or dead, business establishments, events, or locales is entirely coincidental.

ISBN 978-1-338-74673-0

10 9 8 7 6 5 4 3 2   24 25 26 27 28

Printed in the U.S.A.   40

First printing 2024

Book design by Omou Barry

CHAPTER ONE
NO QUARTER

His name was Mr. Kind, which was funny because he wasn't.

And you don't have to just take it from me. There were a few teachers at Ella Fitzgerald Middle School who everyone knew, even if you never took their classes. Ms. Maple, the English teacher who always came to class dressed in character when her class started a new book. Mr. Liu, the science teacher who did experiments in class at least once a week. And Mr. Kind, the math teacher who everyone hated.

It wasn't because of the math-teacher thing. I mean, it was probably a little bit the math-teacher thing. Math teachers get a bad rap, but that's usually personal beef between you, them, and the quadratic equation, not a school-wide dislike that, according to the hottest gossip, even included several teachers.

I generally agreed with the public opinion, but I was

having a conversation with the guy, so I couldn't exactly let it show.

"You want to join the mathletes," he said, squinting at me through his glasses like he had X-ray vision.

It was seventh period—his planning period—so we were alone in his classroom. I was supposed to be in history, but I'd asked Ms. Lopez to let me leave a few minutes early to talk to him. He was a little older than my dad. Square-faced, with a bristly, graying mustache that crinkled as he pushed his lips together to suss me out. His desk was stacked neatly with tests and assignments, separated by class period, and behind it hung a flag that seemed more like it belonged in my history class. It was a red banner with three pointed ends, stamped with a yellow sun that was shooting out rays.

I glanced up at the flag, and he followed my eyes.

"Ah, you've noticed the oriflamme," he said, sounding extremely pleased with himself.

I mean, it was a giant red-and-yellow banner hung behind him like something out of *Game of Thrones*—I don't know how I was supposed to miss it—but I just nodded.

"Do you know what it means?"

"No," I said, lying through my teeth. Like I said, Mr. Kind had a reputation. I'd heard about that flag within two weeks of starting at the Fitz. And, even if I hadn't, I'd for sure know about it by now.

He was our target, after all.

The job had just come in earlier that morning, a referral from David. Officially, David was my peer counselor, but unofficially, he was more like my shrink—and even more unofficially, he was a great source of information on people who needed to be helped. Specifically, people who needed to be helped in ways that didn't exactly line up with the official school code of conduct.

Usually, we worked with a lot more prep time than the four periods between my lunch period and final bell, but this was an emergency.

"It's one of my clients, Sienna Chase," David had said when he tracked me down during lunch. "Eighth grader. You might have seen her around."

I had. I'd never talked to her, but if our school had main characters, she'd have been one. She treated the hallways like her own personal runway, and she never missed a photo op. I thought it was a bit much, but, to her credit, people seemed to like her.

"She actually has a lot of focus when it comes to things she cares about, but schoolwork doesn't always make the list—especially last semester, since she was campaigning hard to get a nomination for Snow Princess—you know, for the winter formal. We've been working on setting goals, though, and she was making a lot of progress."

That progress had apparently culminated in a big push to study for her winter midterms—midterms that had been moved to post winter break since everything had gotten snowed out in mid-December. It was the first week of January now, and we were back from break.

"Isn't that a good thing?" I'd asked. "Extra days to study?"

"It would have been," David had agreed. "But last night, her little sister's appendix burst. Had to be rushed to the hospital. She was up all night worried sick. She came in to take this test on no sleep, while her sister was still in surgery, and when she asked if she could take the test another day . . ."

"Have you ever heard the phrase *no quarter*?" Mr. Kind

asked me, not waiting for my response before he said, "In battles, sometimes the winning side would take prisoners for ransom. Sometimes they wouldn't. That's what *no quarter* means. Take no prisoners. In medieval times, the French would raise the oriflamme in battle when they meant to give no quarter."

Personally, I thought it was kind of messed up to have a flag that basically meant "Make sure to kill everybody" hanging up in a middle school math class, but clearly, he didn't see the problem with it.

"That's how I run my classroom, and that's how I run the mathletes, because that's how life is. Take no prisoners. And it's important to learn that now."

I killed a twitch of annoyance on my lips. I hated that. *Hey, kids, life is harsh so I'm going to make it harsher!* What kind of twisted logic was that? It was that no-quarter policy that he had used to shut down Sienna when she asked to reschedule her test. It was why he had the reputation as the most hated teacher at school—a title he seemed to hold with pride.

It was also what was going to save Sienna, if I had anything to say about it.

I pushed all my feelings about Mr. Kind deep down in a ball in my stomach and said, "I know being a mathlete isn't easy, but I like math and I'm good at it."

He made a little unimpressed sound. "You're going to have to do more than just like it if you want to cut it here," he said, like we were talking about the actual Olympics and not the math Olympics. "But, if you think you've got the right stuff, you're welcome to apply."

He grabbed the saddlebag on the floor next to him, opened it up, and pulled out a flyer. "Here's the information. You'll have to take a qualifying exam."

I reached for the flyer. "Thanks, I—" But the sentence was cut off by my elbow hitting the stack of exams at the corner of the table, sending them sailing toward the floor.

"Shoot! Sorry!" I dropped to my knees and began scrambling to pick them up. "Stay there, I got it."

I scanned the upper-right corner for names as I grabbed the unmarked exams. Rachel Douglas. Sammy Baxter. Ah! Sienna Chase. I slid that test to the front and stacked the rest of the exams behind it. I stayed down there until the bell rang and then stayed down for a couple seconds more.

When I popped up with the tests, he was already standing and sliding the other periods' tests into his saddlebag. I handed him my stack, and he slid it in at the front and pulled the flap shut.

I took the flyer and made for the door.

"I'll for sure look this over. Thanks, Mr. Kind!"

When I walked into the hall, kids were already starting to pour out of their classrooms, eager to get the heck out of Dodge ASAP. I made a beeline for the water fountain and pretended to drink. My part of the job was over, but I still had to make sure everyone else did their part.

Not that I didn't trust them—I had a pretty awesome team.

And, right on cue, I saw one member rounding the corner. Our Face: Audrey Valentine. Even in game mode, it was hard not to smile when I saw her. Her smiles were contagious in the same way that yawns were. They were to me, anyway. She was walking down the hall with one of her Drama Club friends, Kelly.

She walked past me like she hadn't seen me, but I could tell she had. I wouldn't be able to tell you exactly how I knew, but I did. When you work with someone long enough you can sense their tells. Not that I'd worked with Audrey for very long—only since November—but we were already on the same page.

She started walking just a bit faster—if I was at the fountain, then it meant that Mr. Kind was following behind soon. Kelly matched her pace, and right as Mr. Kind walked out, saddlebag slung across his shoulder, Audrey was approaching, talking a bit louder than necessary for a private conversation between her and Kelly.

"I just don't believe in negative numbers," Audrey said. "I mean, think about it. They tell us that if you multiply a negative by a negative it becomes positive? How does that make sense? If you owe someone money and then you multiply it, they don't suddenly owe *you* money."

"Huh," said Kelly, the extremely suggestible sixth grader. "I never thought about that before. That makes a lot of sense."

"Right?" said Audrey.

"Wrong, actually," said Mr. Kind as if it wasn't a rhetorical question that hadn't been directed at him at all. As if Audrey didn't know that wasn't how negative numbers worked.

Because, listen. If you want someone to let their guard down, one of the best ways to do it is to get them on their home turf. Sometimes someone's home turf is a place, and sometimes it's a state of mind. And for Mr. Kind? Explaining to people why they were wrong was that state of mind.

He stopped in the middle of the hall, completely blocking traffic and not asking if either girl had somewhere to be. Just 'cause I knew they didn't, didn't mean that he did. Students pressed against them on both sides, but he seemed to not notice them at all.

"There's a big flaw in your logic," he said. "Well, several actually. I want you to picture a number line going in both directions."

As he went into lecture mode, I scanned the hall behind him for the next member of the team. It wasn't hard to spot him, seeing as he stood head and shoulders above everyone else—Monty LaCroix, our Muscle.

He lumbered forward, taking up space in a way that made people avoid him based on pure self-preservation instinct. I used to be one of those people, until last year when I'd learned that he was less grizzly bear, more Care

Bear—once you got past the fact that he was approximately as big as a small bear.

He pushed his way through the crowd, jostling people out of the way. Not with any real force, but enough that it was felt. That is, until he reached Mr. Kind. Mr. Kind was so deep into his speech about the number line that he didn't notice Monty tilt his shoulder back and gently ram into him as he passed.

"Hey!" Mr. Kind said, stopping his mid-hallway lecture for a moment to yell at the retreating Monty. "Watch it!"

Monty didn't look back; he just kept walking.

Mr. Kind huffed. "Kids these days." And then he went straight back into his lecture.

I listened in for another minute or so before making my way to a secluded corner deeper into the school, in the opposite direction that the crowd was moving. Another minute after that, the final member of my team appeared. Conor Reed, the Fingers. Chip-toothed, grinning, and holding Sienna's math test in his left hand.

"Et voilà," he said with a dramatic flourish. "Am I good or am I good?"

He was good. The best, really. I'd known him the

longest out of everyone in the crew. But he was also waving around a stolen test like it was a pom-pom.

"Put that down," I said. "And get rid of it."

He saluted at me. "You got it. Meet you in front of the school after?"

I nodded, and he disappeared into the crowd, probably to the boys' bathroom to shred the test and flush all evidence that it had ever existed.

The plan was honestly pretty simple, at least on paper. And like I said, it hinged on Mr. Kind's favorite two words: *no quarter*.

Because he forced it onto everyone else, but he also applied it to himself—if he lost a test, his policy was that the student got an automatic 100 percent. No retake needed.

Which meant we had to make sure it got lost.

I'd knocked over the tests to get the one we wanted at the top of the pile and create a plausible window for when he could have lost one. Audrey had drawn his attention with her incorrect math and made him less focused on clutching onto his prized saddlebag. The crush of kids in the hallway had desensitized him to touch, and Monty's knock to his left side had distracted him even more while Conor had come in from the other direction and slid the test right out of his bag.

Easy to explain, hard to pull off. And yet, my team had done it without a hitch, with next-to-zero prep time.

It made me feel proud. Since I'd gotten back into the game last year, I'd only taken jobs like this. Jobs I could feel proud of. Jobs I could do without being up sick with guilt. I'd felt good at the end of every job I'd done in the past two months.

But none of those jobs had involved a target with a literal battle flag in their office.

And, I gotta say, that made the victory feel extra good.

CHAPTER TWO
BALANCING ACT

After talking to Conor, I swung by David's office to let him know that Sienna's problem was taken care of.

"Do I want to know how?" he asked as he offered me the jar of lollipops that sat on the front desk.

"You tell me," I said as I scanned the options that were left. My hand hovered over a green apple, but at the last second, I picked a cherry one instead.

He sighed. "I don't think I'm ever going to get used to this."

"Nah, you're doing great." I could get jobs myself if I wanted to—sometimes I did—but David was a great filter. I trusted his judgment—I mean, he knew about everything I'd done, and he wasn't trying to get me condemned to eternal detention. I trusted that he could tell the difference between a bad kid and a kid in a bad situation.

Our first big job, of course, had been the semester before—stealing 100,000 tickets from the downtown Starcade to pay off Conor's debt to Lucas "Lucky" Ford, the pint-size kingpin of the Fitz. Once we'd pulled it off, David (who was vaguely in the loop) started coming to us with other jobs. Since his first referral after the Starcade Job, we'd done about a dozen jobs he'd sent our way, and they'd all been legit. Well, as legit as anything we did could be.

"I won't tell you the nitty-gritty if it'll make you squeamish, but we made Sienna's problem . . . mmm, let's say disappear. You don't have to tell her more than that."

"I don't think I'll tell her anything," David said, rubbing the nonexistent stubble on his chin. "All I said was I'd see if I could talk to someone about it. For all she knows, the problem might have solved itself. I don't want her to count on other problems . . . disappearing."

I smirked. "See? You're a natural." I shoved the lollipop in my pocket. "Anything new?"

He looked at me like I'd asked for a cold glass of pond scum to drink. "Since lunch? DJ, it's the first day back from break. Slow down."

I shrugged. "You know what they say. No rest for the wicked."

"Mm-hm. And are you supposed to be the wicked in this scenario?"

"David, you know what I mean."

"What I *know* is that you've been working nonstop since you started this whole Robin Hood thing. You never turn down a job. You never take a break. Do I need to get you a pamphlet? We have a pamphlet about this."

He started to look for it, but I put up a hand to stop him. "I don't need a pamphlet. And I don't need a break. Even if I did, we just had winter break. I'm all ready to go."

He pressed his lips together like he was thinking before opening his mouth and starting again in his delicate shrink tone that I knew meant he was about to say something I wouldn't like.

"DJ, you know I think this is a good thing you're doing, but have you ever considered that maybe, sometimes, the reason you won't take a break is that you're overcompensating for—"

Before he could finish, my phone buzzed in my pocket.

"Hold that thought," I said, pulling it out so I could

check. It was from Conor: *Yo, are you coming? Auds and Monty are already at her place.*

Right. The group was waiting on me. Conor was probably freezing outside in the January cold. I didn't wanna keep him waiting any longer—and if rushing to meet him got me out of some awkward shrink talk, that was a bonus.

"It's Conor," I said, making for the door. "Sorry, but I gotta go."

"DJ!" he called after me, the way my mom does when I start eating dinner without washing my hands.

But I was already slipping out—with a quick "Tell me if anything else comes in!"

I grabbed my books from my locker and headed out to the front of the school, where Conor was waiting.

"There you are!" he said when he spotted me. He was jittery as ever, but he had been standing out in the cold for several minutes, so for once, it wasn't his fault.

"Sorry, I kinda got caught up in something. Hey, do you have any leads on new jobs? David said he's tapped out for now."

He scoffed. "Oh no. We are not doing this."

"Doing what?"

"Don't act like you don't know what I'm talking about."

"I don't," I said, and I was telling the truth. Conor loved to call me out—it was annoying, but I respected it. But I didn't know what he could be calling me out about. I wasn't hiding anything or lying about anything or avoiding— Oh.

"Ah!" he said, pointing at me. "Your face didn't change, but I can tell when you have a brain ping, DJ."

Out of one awkward conversation and into another.

"I wasn't avoiding it," I said, starting to walk toward Audrey's place and away from Conor's question. "I actually forgot." And, with all the heist stuff, I had. I had been in the zone. But now . . .

Conor fell into lockstep with me, sly smile on his face. "Welllll, now that you remember, and since you're totalllly not avoiding it, we can talk about how you're not gonna blow your shot to ask Audrey to the winter formal this time, right?"

I sighed. "Here we go."

The winter formal had been originally scheduled for late December, right before winter break. And Audrey and I . . . Look, we weren't official-official, but there's no one else I would have asked to the dance, you feel me? And I didn't! But I also didn't ask her.

"She was super bummed, dude!"

"I talked to her before," I said. "She understands."

Everyone at school knew that Conor and I were tight. Conor didn't know how to not stick by me when I was around; and when I wasn't around, he'd transferred schools to be with me. More important, Lucky knew that Conor and I were friends. It was Conor's butt I'd saved during the Starcade Job, after all. And I was pretty sure Lucky knew about Monty, too. Standing around and looking menacing was the number one task we assigned him on jobs, and if you were keeping track of me like Lucky was, he'd be pretty hard to miss. But Audrey's skills were all in finesse. She flew under the radar like a fighter jet and feigned innocence like a pro, even when she was calling attention to herself. Conor, Monty, and I had all caught tails on us from Lucky after that first job, and I'd assumed Audrey had, too, but it seemed like I'd been wrong. The three of us occasionally got roughed up by Lucky's goons, but she never did. She'd managed to stay clean, and I intended to keep it that way.

"Just because she understands doesn't mean she wasn't super bummed."

"She wasn't . . . *super* bummed."

Audrey was our Face, which meant that she was really good at hiding her emotions, but she always let me know how she felt when we talked.

"I know it's technically safer for me," she'd said. "And it makes me more useful to the team if people don't know I'm part of it. That doesn't mean I don't wish we could go. But I guess I knew you were gonna say this. It's the same at school."

Y'all know I'm a big believer in a good poker face, but the lack of one, when properly deployed, can be just as effective. And man, her understanding smile paired with the disappointed dip of her shoulders killed me. I loved hanging out with Audrey. We went to her house after school almost every day! And it wasn't like she didn't have other friends—she was hardly lonely. But the fact that it was what was best for the team didn't make the fact that we couldn't casually hang out at school, well, not a bummer.

But then a huge snowstorm had blown through and the dance got canceled along with everything else. Yesterday, it was announced that the dance was rescheduled for the last Saturday in January. Conor thought it was a sign—a divine do-over. I was dreading having to hear and ignore reminders to buy tickets and nominate candidates for Snow Prince and Princess every day again for another three weeks.

"Dude," Conor said, "the only reason she's not mad at you is 'cause she likes you, and that's why you should go with her. She doesn't care if it's a little risky!"

"But I do," I said. "Besides, middle school dances aren't that great. Everyone just stands around awkwardly and doesn't dance. We'll have more fun if we don't go and just watch movies or something. Anyway, what do you know?"

"I know you should go to the dance with Audrey," he shot back. "Or at least the pre-dance carnival the Thursday before."

He'd been excited about the carnival since even before break. The high school his older sister, Bethany, went to had put on their own winter carnival right before everything had been snowed out, which seemed to have pumped up his excitement for our own to the max.

"It sounds awesome! We get to miss class. And the food is going to be from the same places the high school got their food from—which I know is super awesome from the leftovers I swiped from Beth. It's gonna have a lot of the same games and prizes, too! And we collected enough cans for the food drive before break, so there's gonna be a surprise!"

"You know I don't like surprises, Conor."

Of course that didn't stop him from bugging me about the dance the rest of the way to Audrey's place, but I gave him a good enough death stare before I rang the doorbell that he knocked it off before Audrey came to answer it.

"Perfect timing!" Audrey said as she opened the door and let the two of us in. "Monty just finished making chicken nuggets."

"Sweet!" Conor said, knocking fists with her as he beelined for the kitchen. "Dibs on any burned ones!"

Audrey snorted as she watched him go, then turned back to me. "He's so weird."

"Yeah," I said. "He came that way, but I think he's getting weirder."

"I mean, who isn't? Oh!"

She suddenly grabbed my hand, and my heart skipped a beat like always. I would have thought that it would have calmed down by now, but if anything, it'd gotten worse.

Not that it was a bad thing. When she brought my hand up to eye level and looked at my nails, I realized why she'd done it.

"Oh yeah. I was helping my dad with yard stuff yesterday, so the nail polish got all chipped. You can paint them again if you want."

She flashed a big smile. "I got a bottle of blue nail polish for Christmas that I've been dying to use. It'll look so good on you! Come on!"

Personally, I didn't really get it, but Audrey loved painting my nails, and if it made her happy, then I was happy to let her. Plus it made me feel a little better when I missed her at school.

By the time she dragged me into the living room, Monty and Conor were already set up with a whole mess of chicken nuggets, plus ketchup and honey mustard for dipping.

"I made celebration chicken nuggets!" Monty said, gesturing to the plate. Even though it was Audrey's place, he always insisted on helping to make the food. At first we'd tried to share the work. At least Audrey and I had. Conor was more than OK letting Monty be his personal chef.

"If he wants to do it, let him do it!" He was being lazy, but he happened to be right—Monty liked doing stuff for his friends, so just like Audrey with the nail polish, we didn't stop him.

"Thanks, man," I said. "And good work with that shoulder check. You're getting better at not making eye contact with your targets."

He beamed.

"Really, everyone did great on such short notice," I said. "Sorry about that, by the way. I usually wouldn't want to do something with such short notice but—"

"Mr. Kind is the worst?" Conor said through a mouthful of chicken nuggets.

I winced. "Dude, chew. But yes. I really didn't want to let him get away with that."

"He's really mean," said Monty.

"Agreed," said Audrey. "I've been getting warned about that guy since at least fifth grade. I was not about to pass up the chance to get a shot at him, even though I'm totally swamped with makeup work today."

I felt a twinge of guilt. David's words echoed in my head. I might not have felt like I needed a break, but this wasn't a one-man operation. I had to make sure I was thinking about everyone else, too.

"Glad you guys were all so down to jump in," I said. "But I'm going to try to not take anything new for a little bit. I know everyone's schedules are kind of out of whack because of all those snow days, and we should try to get all caught up before we go full throttle again."

Conor swallowed everything in his mouth in one impressive, almost disturbing gulp. "Well," he said in his signature mischievous tone of voice I hated. "If we're gonna be free, then that means you'll be totally free to go to the—"

"Audrey, didn't you say you had nail polish to show me?"

She did a little jump. "Oh, you're right. Sit there."

When she turned to get it from the bag at her side, I mouthed to Conor, "Stop helping."

He threw up his palms and widened his eyes like *Come on, man!*, but went back to normal before Audrey turned and took my hand to start applying the nail polish remover so she could get rid of the old stuff and put on the new.

"Oh, I was just telling Monty. Did you hear about Lucky?" Audrey asked.

"What about him?" Conor asked.

"He wasn't at school today," I pointed out. I'd noticed, but one day right after break wasn't too weird, and I'd been too busy to look into it without a reason.

"Right," Audrey said, pointing the nail polish brush at me. "And I overheard why. Skiing accident."

"He broke his leg," Monty chimed in. "Stuck at home for at least two weeks. Maybe longer."

"Skiing accident?" I said incredulously. "Lucky was skiing? Lucky, who takes PE online, was skiing?"

"Probably why he broke his leg," Conor said, wiping his ketchup-stained fingers on his shirt.

"Good point." If he was out for two weeks, then that meant Mariposa, his second-in-command, would be running everything while he was gone. Collecting any payments, directing any Rocket Boosters, the Lucky Lotto. They were all major operations. Between the Lotto and the various hustles that Lucky got a cut from, she'd be handling more tickets in a day than most kids saw in all of middle school. And the Rocket Boosters system was the ultimate threat. One seemingly innocent announcement over the intercom and you were socially dead for the rest of your middle school life.

Someone who didn't know better might think it was the perfect opportunity to try to get away with some shenanigans. Luckily for us, we knew how much Mariposa and shenanigans didn't mix. Of course, it was an interesting shift in the landscape. Lucky had never been gone for this long since I'd been at the Fitz. Things could happen. Things that innocent bystanders could get caught up in. Things that required—

"Hey."

I was broken out of my thoughts by Audrey waving a hand in front of my eyes. When I focused up, I saw she was staring at me.

"What's up? You look all game face–y."

"Oh, nothing. I'm just thinking about the Lucky thing. Someone might try to take advantage of the situation. Power vacuum and all."

Conor scoffed. "Power vacuum? Mariposa is right there. That's the opposite of a power vacuum. That's a . . ."

"Weakness leaf blower?" Monty suggested.

Audrey snorted, and a drip of nail polish splashed off the brush, barely missing the couch. "What he said. She's more than scary enough to hold down the fort. You know that."

"But—"

She put down the nail polish she was holding and grabbed my shoulder.

"And you just said we were taking a break. That includes you."

"Yeah, man," Conor said. "Just relax and let Audrey do your nails so we can play Rexcellent. She's the only decent competition out of the three of you, and I need to practice for my match tomorrow. Like, she's still going to lose, but a little bit slower than you two would."

She stuck her tongue out at him and then turned back to me, smiling slightly. "I know your brain doesn't shut off, but you've been in go-time mode all day and—"

And we hadn't gotten to hang out. Not really. We'd seen each other more than usual, but that was just planning.

"And you're right," I said. It's hard for me to turn off my brain, like she said, but I tried my best to at least put it on ice. It was one thing to not hang out with her during school, but if I was also talking shop the entire time I was in her living room, then I would be totally out of pocket and I would have to admit to David that I needed his stupid pamphlet.

"Sorry, I'll chill. Hey, tell me about choir. Is Brent still all twisted that you got that solo at the winter concert instead of him?"

That got her going. She immediately launched into the latest installment of the *Star Wars*–length choir class drama saga she'd been filling us in on. The way Audrey told a story, it was almost enough to keep my mind off work.

Almost.

CHAPTER THREE
DINO-MITE

The next day, when I got to school, my good buddy Curtis was waiting for me at the drop-off loop. Which would have been fine except for the fact that I didn't have a good buddy named Curtis.

That didn't stop him from slinging a beefy arm around me as soon as I stepped onto school grounds, a smile plastered on his pasty white face.

"Hey, DJ," he said, fingertips digging into my shoulder. "You're here early. Wanna grab breakfast?"

"Nah, I have places to be," I said, pointlessly attempting to shrug his arm off. With the vise grip he had on me, I wasn't going anywhere except for exactly where he wanted me to go, a fact he made clear as he chuckled like I'd made a joke and started walking us toward the cafeteria.

Because here was the thing: I didn't have a good buddy named Curtis, but Mariposa did.

Or whatever someone like Mariposa had instead of friends. Minions, I guess.

She wasn't the kind of person who needed muscle to be intimidating, but that didn't stop her from calling in reinforcements when she wanted to send an extra-pointed message.

Curtis strong-armed me to the table in the corner of the cafeteria where Mariposa was conducting business.

Her eyes always carried a kind of icy quality, but I could tell as we approached her that the blast chiller was up to maximum. There was a little blond boy sitting across from her who must have been a sixth grader, but he was so small I would have believed it if I'd been told he was a third grader.

I couldn't hear what she was saying to him, but the interaction reminded me of the time I'd seen a boa constrictor being fed live mice at the zoo. Except the mice didn't squirm nearly as much.

She noticed us approaching, then turned back to the kid, whose squeaky voice cut through the dull roar in the cafeteria.

"But that's all the sugar I get all day!" he pleaded. "My parents don't believe in sugar. They give out toothbrushes for Halloween!"

Her face twitched with a flicker of disgust but not an ounce of sympathy. "Well, you should have thought about that before you went into debt with Lucky just to blow it all on Fun Dip. Now, do we have a deal, or will we be exploring alternate payment options?"

As she said that, Curtis rammed into the kid, just hard enough to spook him. The kid practically jumped out of his skin, and Curtis clamped down on his shoulder.

"Easy, little guy," he said with a relaxed grin. "Just an accident. Why so jumpy?"

"Do we have a deal?" Mariposa repeated with a tone that said she wouldn't ask again.

"Deal," the kid said quickly, sliding over something to her that I didn't quite see before jumping up again and vacating the premises as quickly as his little legs would take him. Mouse lives to see another day.

As he scurried away, Curtis pushed me down into his empty spot.

I frowned at him and glanced over at Mariposa. "You

can tell your guy I know how to sit down. Just like I knew last time."

She flicked her eyes up at Curtis, and he backed up, but just a bit.

"DJ," she said, making my name alone sound like some kind of accusation.

"Mariposa," I said in return, keeping my voice casual. "Pretty short notice for an appointment. I should feel honored. Especially since you're pulling double duty with Lucky gone. You must be busy."

"I am," she said curtly, "so I'll keep this short. Do you happen to know why the best Face in the entire sixth grade has suddenly decided he's more interested in preparing for the spring musical than running jobs for us?"

I sure did. That had been another referral from David. A naturally gifted Face looking for an alternate outlet—one Audrey had provided with a gentle nudge into musical theater. But I wasn't about to tell Mariposa that. Instead, I gave her my best doe eyes.

"I dunno. Maybe he figured it would look better on his high school résumé?"

Oh, she did not like that. She glanced again at Curtis,

who closed the small gap between us so I could feel his breath on my ear.

"So you're saying you and your . . . *people* didn't have anything to do with this?"

I shrugged. "I don't tell people what to do. People can make their own decisions."

"Hmm." She studied me carefully before speaking again. "Well, I suggest you start making yours a little more carefully. Because messing with our operations is a dangerous game, and your little fail-safe won't protect you forever."

I swatted at the queasy fluttering in my stomach sparked by the threat. The only thing we had keeping Lucky and Mariposa from strong-arming us into becoming their minions was an ultimatum to tank the value of the Starcade tickets they used to run the school, an ultimatum that was about 50 percent bluff. If they realized that, our already shaky position would get a lot shakier.

But I just fell back on my motto: Jumpy insides, calm outsides.

"I'll keep that in mind. Now, do you wanna split an order of French toast sticks or are we done here?"

She gave me a glare that was answer enough, and I hopped out of my seat—not as quickly as mouse boy but pretty quickly.

I mean, I couldn't miss Conor's big race.

Now you're probably thinking: *Hey, wasn't Conor super, perma-mega banned from Lucky's racing derby circuit until the heat death of the universe?* And you'd be correct. Conor was absolutely persona non grata for any Lucky-run operations. But that wasn't the only racing circuit in town.

After I'd delivered Conor's list of Rexcellent Racers cheats to Mariposa so she could hack-proof any future tournaments Lucky ran, she'd done something I hadn't expected. She'd opened a new racing circuit, no-holds-barred, all cheats allowed. Well, technically *she* hadn't. Her cousin Miguel hosted it and ran the day-to-day. But it was pretty clear to me that the operation had Mariposa's fingerprints all over it. He was always able to secure a computer lab for his "Technology Enthusiast Club" meetings—a snap with Mariposa's front office connections. And the timing lined up with when we tipped her off on the codes. I'd honestly been a little nervous that Conor jumping into the TEC scene would set her off, but it hadn't been an issue. She'd never dragged me or him in to call us out for it. My guess? He was just too good to keep out without affecting the bottom line.

TEC matches weren't for everyone, but there were enough people who liked the chaos of a cheating-allowed game to make it a solid revenue stream in its own right, and an even bigger stream in organized betting on the winners.

When I got to the computer lab, the door opened before I could touch the knob.

"DJ," Conor said, ushering me in and closing the door behind us. "You made it!"

"Of course," I said. "I'm not late for things. That's you, remember?"

He elbowed me in the ribs but smiled, keeping an eye out in the hall through the window as he did. Technically, nothing about TEC matches were against school rules—phones were allowed as long as it wasn't class time, and the room was properly booked. But it was the kind of thing that had the potential to become against the rules if too many people knew about it, so someone always kept watch while matches were happening.

"I'm on after Cat Fight Fight Club," Conor said. "But that should be over soon."

Sure enough, when I looked up at the projection on the whiteboard, I saw a cartoon Russian blue kitty in martial arts gear absolutely pummeling a cyborg tabby cat into the corner of the screen.

Cat Fight was a new mobile game by the same team that'd made Rexcellent—an arcade-style beat-'em-up where you picked an adorable kitty fighter to smack down your opponent until they were down for the count and coughing up hairballs. It wasn't as popular as Rexcellent yet, but it was getting there. And despite its cute characters, it had a pretty active hacking community dedicated to making these kitties' claws even sharper.

At the front of the stage, near the screen, Miguel was giving a play-by-play. His glasses were in his hand, pointing at the screen like he couldn't believe what he was seeing.

"She's got him pinned! He can't even fight back! She's outboxing the boxer!"

She was Cami from the Trading Post, sitting in front of one of the computers but laser focused on her phone. Her opponent, Jamie, was frantically tapping at his screen, trying to figure a way out of the corner he was literally being boxed into, but it was pointless. Within a few seconds, he was KO'd and Cami raised her fist triumphantly. So did Conor.

I squinted at him. "Since when are you and Cami friends?"

"Who said we were friends?" said Conor. "I just put a big bet on her winning in under thirty."

I sighed. "You have a problem, dude."

"Only if Cami suddenly gets bad at Cat Fight!" he said as he sauntered over to take her place in the hot seat. As he left the door, Jamie took over his watch, hiding his sulkiness but not very well.

"What a match!" Miguel said, sliding his glasses back onto his face. "We'll definitely have to do more Cat Fight next time. But time for the main event. Dino Death Match!"

The small crowd gathered in the room cheered. Cat Fight may have been gaining in popularity, but Rexcellent was still top dog.

"We only have a few minutes before the bell, so it's a good thing our competitors are so quick! In the T-Wrecks we have our returning champion, Conor! And once again, challenging him, we have Ambrose in the Tricera-Tank!"

Ambrose was a bit of a weird person to see at a TEC match. Honestly, he was weird to see anywhere on campus because he was one of those kids who came to school wearing a dress shirt and tie. Every day. Even during the summer, according to Audrey. But he was especially weird to see at something as low-key sketchy as a TEC match. You would expect him to be hanging with Mr. Kind and the mathletes or something. But despite his aesthetic, he was very into gaming. He'd actually come away with second place in Lucky's tournament last year but couldn't quite clinch it.

That second-place streak had continued once TEC matches had started and Conor became the one to beat.

Ambrose scowled at Conor and adjusted his tie as he sat down. "I still can't believe you main the T-Wrecks. That's so basic."

Conor snorted. "I can't believe I've smoked you with the same car twelve times in a row. Oh, wait, I totally can!"

"All right, all right, settle down," said Miguel. "If you want to have a catfight, sign up for that game next time. Get into the game lobby. We don't have all day."

Ambrose opened his mouth again like he wanted to say something but closed it with a little smile and started fiddling with his phone. So did Conor, and soon they were set up.

"Cretaceous Crater Course!" Miguel announced once the randomized spinner chose it. "Watch out for lava!"

"Don't need to with a perma–heat shield," Conor said smugly. Ambrose ignored him and gripped his phone tighter.

On the screen a countdown started—*3, 2, 1*—and then a chorus of dino noises, and the competitors set off. Conor's car raced forward and hit the first power-up in his path—a speed boost. But on contact it changed from blue to red. A heat shield. Then he gunned it and headed right through the upcoming lava flow instead of trying to swerve around it.

I took my eyes off the match and looked at the door. This was not Conor's first rodeo. I was there for moral support, but I'd seen this before. I was more interested in keeping another set of eyes on the door to make sure this wasn't his *last* victory.

I let the noises from the match fade into the background

until I heard "What the—?" from Conor, which made me turn. Ambrose was ramming into him with his Tricera-Tank, and it didn't look like he was taking any heat damage.

"A damage booster stacked on a heat shield during the first lap!" Miguel said. "That's pretty tricky!"

"Not tricky enough," Conor mumbled under his breath as he swiped at his screen. There was a stutter on-screen as his car glitched out of reach of Ambrose's car and sped forward. "Let's see you shield this." A meteor missile launched out of the back of his car and locked on to Ambrose's.

Ambrose smirked without looking up. On-screen, his car glitched forward as well and appeared right next to Conor's.

Conor's eyes went wide. He turned to look at Ambrose and then at me.

"Eyes on the road!" I said, pointing back at the screen.

"But—"

"Incoming!" Jamie called from the door suddenly.

The room sprang into action. Phones into pockets. Loose tickets hidden away. Video on-screen switched to a report on the latest model of the hottest game console. I slid into one of the chairs and pretended to be very invested.

A second later, the door opened and in walked Caroline Spitz. She was a Space Cadet—and, no, that's not an insult. That's what they were actually called and they *liked it*. The program had started up the year before Rocket Boosters. It started out as a hall monitor program, but they also did things like running messages for the front office and helping out with events. They didn't have *that* much power, and everyone knew that, but they had *enough* power that dealing with them was better avoided—especially Caro. She was the head cadet, which was wild because that wasn't even a position that had existed before she'd lobbied for it.

She sized up the room, eyes settling on Conor for a second too long before stopping on Miguel.

"Hey, Caro," he said smoothly, pausing the video he'd literally just started. "Are you joining TEC?"

She scoffed as if being a glorified errand girl was somehow better than being a tech geek and said, "No. I just came in here to say you were being loud. I can hear you from outside."

"My bad," said Miguel. "We're just super excited about tech. Right, guys?"

Everyone in the room nodded, and to be fair, it wasn't

a lie exactly. Cheating at mobile games wasn't *not* tech, and everyone in the room was pretty invested in that for various reasons.

"But we'll keep it down. Sorry, Caro."

She gave him a curt nod, her blond fringe bobbing forward. I looked down so she didn't see me roll my eyes. There's only so much even my poker face can handle.

Once she was gone, Miguel checked the wall clock. "Shoot. Not enough time to finish the match. We'll have to reschedule."

A groan rolled through the group like thunder, but he held up his hands.

"Hey, hey, hey. I'm not gonna have anyone complaining to me that one of my matches was unfair. Not when so many tickets are on the line. Conor, Ambrose, see me at lunch so we can reschedule. If anyone has any complaints, they can talk to me."

The bell rang, adding a punch of finality to his statement, and everyone grudgingly got up to leave.

Ambrose slung his backpack over his shoulder and glanced at Conor. "You got lucky. But next time, Caro won't show up to save you."

"Uh, I think it's still twelve–zero, dude," Conor said, holding up his hand in a circle, which he shoved in Ambrose's face. "You can trash-talk me when you actually win one."

He watched Ambrose leave, waited a beat, and then turned to me.

"He's cheating."

I searched Conor's face to see what I was missing. "Uh . . . yeah. Everyone is. Isn't that the point?"

"No!" Conor said, throwing his arms up. Then he remembered there were still other people in the room, and he dropped his voice to just above a whisper. "He's cheating using *my* cheats."

"What do you mean?"

"The extra power-ups and that glitch move? Those are mine!"

I shook my head. "Come on, dude. Just because he's getting better—"

"He's not getting better," Conor insisted. "He's using my cheats! I can tell. You saw how smug he was."

"He's always smug. He's Ambrose."

"Yeah, but he was extra smug! And what, did he just get that good at modding the game overnight?"

"He had all break," I pointed out. "He could have just watched a lot of YouTube tutorials."

"I know my cheats," Conor said, crossing his arms. "That little stutter before it activates? That's my signature! That's how I know if people are jacking my code!"

I really couldn't argue with that. Conor was the tech-savvy one in the crew. I was used to just taking his word on things like this. But I also knew he didn't always think things all the way through. I didn't want him to jump to conclusions.

"OK," I said. "Tell Miguel you're busy for the next couple of weeks so you can't do a rematch yet. That will give us some time to look into it. I'll see what I can find out."

"Cool," he said, "because if I lose to Ambrose on my own hacks, I promise you, I will figure out how to transfer schools again."

CHAPTER FOUR
DÉJÀ VU

After I left Conor, I swung by Audrey's locker and slipped in the cherry lollipop I'd gotten from David. I knew she had a science test she was worried about, so I'd snagged the lollipop for her. The rest of the day was busy with makeup work but pretty uneventful.

When the final bell rang, I hung out in my classroom for a while before making a beeline for my locker. Mine is in the main hallway, which means it's always super crowded as soon as the bell rings. I like to wait until it clears up if I can spare the time.

I keyed in my locker combo, and as the door swung open, a slip of paper fell out. I automatically reached out my hand to catch it but stopped short as I realized it was Tuesday. Lucky Lotto slips—entry forms to Lucky's weekly ticket lottery—went out on Mondays, and I'd already thrown mine away. And this was the wrong color, too, I noticed as it fell past my hand toward the floor. This was a ripped piece of notebook paper, not his special green form.

I might have scooped it up and tossed it in the nearest trash can without looking at it if not for what happened when it hit the ground.

It pinged.

Paper doesn't ping.

If the hallway had been mobbed by loud students, exiting the premises as quickly as they were able to, I probably would have missed it.

I frowned. That was weird. Had something else fallen out with this stray piece of notebook paper?

As I picked it up, I could feel that there was something stuck to the back of it, but there was also writing on it, which I read first. It was in shaky but not unreadable pencil—just three letters, circled and crossed out: *BPS*.

BPS? I'd never heard of a BPS. What did it mean? Why was it crossed out? And what was it doing in my locker? When I flipped the note, I was even more confused. Taped to the back was a pencil. Well, about half a pencil anyway. It was about three inches long from eraser to splintered end and classic school-pencil yellow. But something was missing, besides the rest of the pencil. Where there was usually a *No. 2*, there was instead a *No. 1*.

A number one pencil? I'd never seen a number one pencil in my life. Honestly, it had never crossed my mind that they might be a thing, but now that I was thinking about it, it made sense. A number two always implies that there's a number one out there somewhere.

Which explained why the pencil existed but not why it was in my locker attached to a note with the letters *BPS* circled and crossed out.

I checked over my shoulder, not really expecting to see anyone. Whoever'd slipped it into my locker must have been long gone. Still, I felt tense. I didn't know what *BPS* meant, but a note with something crossed out isn't usually friendly unless it's a shopping list, you know? What if it was a threat? But threats usually worked better when you knew what they meant. What was this telling me to do . . . or not do? And it didn't even have to be a threat. It could be a message or a warning or—

I froze as a neatly trimmed Afro disappeared down a corner. A strangely familiar Afro. I felt a sudden wave of déjà vu, similar to Conor's sudden reappearance in my cafeteria last semester.

It couldn't be, could it? He didn't go to this school. He didn't go to middle school anymore, *period*. But I'd hung out with him so much. It was like a song you recognize from the first note—I knew the back of that head.

I made a U-turn and raced down the hall, stopping right before he opened a door, and yelled, "Malik?"

The figure stopped and turned. He was a little taller than the last time I'd seen him, and he was wearing a weird outfit that looked halfway between a girl's one-piece swimsuit and overalls, but it was unmistakably him.

"Darius James," he said with a grin. "Small world."

The last time I'd talked to Malik, I'd been telling him we couldn't talk again. Not because I had beef with him or anything. In fact, I'd never had a problem with him—as long as he got paid, he worked fine with anyone. He was our Face back at Grover—outside of Audrey, the best I'd ever worked with. We'd just finished our last job—what I had thought was my actual last job, code-named Itsy-Bitsy Spider.

Except the spider hadn't been very itsy-bitsy, and I'd actually sent a grown man into a panic attack and myself into a guilt spiral that had ended with me transferring schools and coming to the Fitz. I'd broken up the crew after that. Gone radio silent and swore to never do another job again. And then, of course, Conor had shown up at my new school, and that plan had gone down the tubes.

But it couldn't be happening again. Could it? In fact, I knew it couldn't. Malik wasn't even in middle school anymore. We were the same age, but last I'd heard, he'd skipped two grades and was now a freshman at a local high school. So, what was he doing back at a middle school—and not even his own? It felt kind of conceited to assume it had to do with me, but I couldn't think of any other reason he could be around.

"Long time no see," he said, walking up to me and giving my arm a light punch. "Funny seeing you here."

"Is it?" I said. "I go here. I should be saying that to you. Aren't you in high school now?"

He grinned. "Yup, yup. Your boy is a freshman."

I hadn't been surprised when I'd heard the news. He wasn't a planner like me, so he needed direction on jobs, but when it came to book smarts, he was just as much honor roll material as I was.

"Well, congrats," I said. "And don't take this the wrong way, but what the heck are you doing here?" I didn't trust coincidences on a good day, and I especially didn't trust them in the form of shady old business associates in the middle of my new school.

He laughed. "Wrestling practice, bro."

I squinted at him. "Wrestling practice? You don't wrestle."

"I do now," he said. "Why do you think I'm dressed like this? For fun?"

I pressed my lips together. I had been wondering about the getup. And I guessed he could have picked up a new interest in the past seven months, but it still felt . . . off.

"I can't wrestle with the high school kids," he said. "Above my weight class. So I come here. Well, I just started. Gotta do something to keep myself busy now that I'm retired."

My eyes flicked around to make sure we were alone, and he laughed again.

"Oh, relax. No one's eavesdropping. You were always so paranoid. But it did keep us out of trouble, so I can't be mad about it. Speaking of trouble, you got anything fun happening here?"

"I already told you back at the Grove," I said firmly. "I'm out."

He winked at me. "Suuuure. I got you."

Something about the way he said it ticked me off. I mean, I was lying, but he didn't know that. Well, maybe he did. Face skills. But that wasn't what it felt like. It felt like he was saying I couldn't quit. Like I couldn't change. And I *had* changed. At least I thought I had. I was still doing the same things but for different reasons. Better ones. That counted, right?

I tried to shake the feeling. His opinion didn't matter. Only my actions mattered, and they were better now. At least I hoped so. I made a mental note to book an appointment with David.

Malik didn't seem to notice that I was playing mental Twister as he casually slid his hand into his pocket and pulled out a pack of gum. He grabbed two sticks, and at first I thought he was going to offer one to me. But instead, he unwrapped them both and crammed them into his mouth.

"Oh," he said, glancing at me. "You want one?"

"No," I said, "I'm good."

And so was he, apparently. Malik had a gum-chewing

habit—one he couldn't break even when he'd gotten braces in sixth grade. The braces were gone now, and the habit was as sticky as ever. But there was a thing about Malik I'd noticed but never commented on. He always chewed sticks of gum one after the other. It was wild to watch. But he never chewed more than a stick at a time—except after jobs.

"Hey," I said. "I gotta go. Nice seeing you, though."

"Yeah," he said. "When you see him, tell Conor I said hey." He punched my shoulder and headed off.

I waited a beat for him to walk off and then booked it for the entrance, where my ride was waiting. As I made it to the pickup loop, Conor's sister Bethany poked her head out her car window.

"Hey, DJ! There you are! Hop in so I can get you home."

"Hey, Beth," I said. "Would it be OK if I came over instead? We have a *group project* we need to work on, and the deadline is earlier than I expected."

At the words *group project*, Conor perked up. So did Bethany, but she only said, "Sure," in a tone that implied she didn't fully believe my story but also didn't care enough to call me out. She cranked up the radio and started cruising while Conor raised an eyebrow at me.

"What's up with the project?" he asked.

"I'll tell you when we get to your place," I said.

Bethany was pretty willing to turn a blind eye to our shenanigans, but I knew older-sister responsibilities kicked in at a certain point, and I didn't want to find the line.

The second we were behind Conor's bedroom door he said, "Dude, you're freaking out. Well, you're not freaking out, but you're doing the DJ version of it. What's up?"

"Malik," I said. "Right after we split up, I saw him in the hall."

His eyebrows shot up to his hairline. "Malik from the Grove?"

"What other Malik would I be talking about?"

"Yeah, I know, just—isn't he in high school? What was he doing there?"

"He said wrestling, but I don't believe him. Too much of a coincidence for him to just randomly be here in the middle of all the rest of this mess. And when he pulled out his gum? Two sticks!"

Conor paused like he was expecting me to say more. "Which means?"

"Conor! He only does that when he's finished a job. Am I the only one who noticed?"

"Usually, yeah."

I groaned.

"Hey, chill," Conor said before plopping down onto his bed. "So, what do you think he was doing there?"

"I'm not sure," I said. "But something is up. The guy is a magnet for trouble. We don't see him for months, and then all of a sudden, he shows up at our school and says he's getting into wrestling for the first time in his life? I don't buy it. You? Sure. Him? No way."

"Maybe someone wanted him to do Face work?" Conor suggested. "We did put that one sixth grader out of commission."

"Could be, but that seems like overkill. Last year, when we needed a Face—and needed one bad—we didn't call him in, we got Audrey."

"Hmm. Maybe something more specialized, then? He helped me with tech sometimes," Conor pointed out. "Like when we cracked the school's LED display board out front or when we were rigging that election or—" His eyes suddenly went wide.

"What?" I asked.

"Dino Death Match! Do you think he's the one helping Ambrose?"

I frowned. "I wouldn't put it past him. But what I wanna know is how Ambrose would even know Malik. Oh! And I almost forgot. I found this in my locker right before I saw him."

I dug into my pocket and pulled out the note and the pencil.

Conor turned the pencil over in his hand. "A broken pencil?"

"Look at the number," I said.

"Weird. I never knew number one pencils existed."

"Neither did I," I said.

He checked out the note. "*BPS*. Do you know what that stands for?"

"Nope."

"Is this Malik's handwriting?"

"Not sure," I said. "We can check our last yearbook where he signed and compare. But that still doesn't explain what *BPS* means. Or why it's crossed out. Or what kind of message whoever sent this is trying to get across. And . . ."

"And?" Conor prompted.

I thought about mentioning the uneasy feeling that was still bubbling in my stomach from Malik scoffing at the thought of my retirement but decided against it. Conor didn't need to know about that. I could deal with it myself.

"And we need to figure it out as fast as we can," I said instead. "We don't know if the two are connected, but if they are, you'll have your answer, and, if they're not, Malik is a part of something that's happening right under our noses."

"Yikes," Conor said. "He has so much dirt on us."

That thought had been floating around in the back of my mind, too. If he wanted to go toe-to-toe with us, he was in a better position than most. The Spider Job alone was probably enough to get me expelled. But that was all the more reason to figure out if he was up to something.

"We'll have to be careful," I agreed. "And work as fast as we can. You find the yearbook; I'll start trying to figure out what's up with this note."

"A good old-fashioned mystery," Conor said, getting up to grab the yearbook from his bookshelf. "Lemme text Audrey and Monty. If they help then—"

"No!"

He froze mid reach and turned to look at me head-on, raising a curious eyebrow.

"No?"

"Ah, I mean, we should leave them out of it. They're busy. And this is our baggage from our old school, so, you know. No reason to get them wrapped into it."

He snorted. "Are you sure you just don't wanna get in trouble with Audrey for not taking a break after you said you would?"

"No."

Which was the truth. It wasn't *just* that.

I broke eye contact with him before he could call me out again.

"Listen, we'll call them in if we need to, but, if we do this fast, we won't need to. Let's get to work."

CHAPTER FIVE
ANOTHER PIECE

Conor and I did as much research as we could, but it didn't turn up much.

The handwriting on the note didn't match Malik's "Take it easy Con-Man" in Conor's sixth-grade yearbook and a quick look on his social media profiles showed that he *was* friends with members of our wrestling team. But handwriting could be faked and I 100 percent believed he would legitimately join a wrestling team for an illegitimate reason, so we tried figuring out the note itself.

Conor's best guess was that BPS stood for someone's initials—first, middle, and last. We ran through everyone we knew at school who might fit, but we didn't know everyone who went to our school, and, even with the kids we did know, we didn't know most of their middle initials.

I did some googling for what else the letters might stand for, but I didn't find anything useful. I didn't think anyone at our school was involved with Buffalo Public Schools or the Board of Pharmacy Specialties.

After a couple of hours, we called it quits for the day. The more we worked on it, the more it felt like we were chasing shadows. The note could mean anything. More important, it could mean nothing. My natural suspicion made it hard for me to believe that Malik wasn't connected to the mysterious note, and I still felt like he was up to *something*, but it was entirely possible the two things were unrelated. Not every scam that happened was somehow related to me.

The note could have been a random doodle shoved in a random locker because the kid who wrote it was too lazy to find a trash can. The pencil thing was weirder, but that didn't mean anything suspicious was going on, necessarily. A middle school is literally a building full of kids doing weird stuff for no reason.

That night, as I lay in bed, I started second-guessing the idea that Malik was even involved in anything. Was it possible that he had actually just gotten really into wrestling?

Him being around pinged my spidey-sense but was what I was feeling suspicion or was it just that I didn't like the reminder of the life I'd tried to leave behind?

I decided to ask Conor what he thought at lunch the next day. If there was anyone I could trust to tell me that I was being ridiculous, it was him. In the meantime, I'd try to keep my mind off it. I had promised Audrey I'd take a break after all.

The next day, during homeroom, I was still feeling uneasy about the whole situation, so I paid attention to the morning announcements to have something to focus on besides my own thoughts.

Lacey and Brad were the two head anchors for the morning announcement. While both of them were good at their jobs, only Lacey was secretly in the pocket of Mariposa, pulling the trigger on any Rocket Booster announcements Lucky ordered.

Unsurprisingly, there weren't any Rocket Booster announcements that day—as scary as they were, they were also pretty rare.

Brad finished a story about some second-string basketball player who got off the bench and scored a bunch of points, and then Lacey was up for an interview with the student body president, Tessa McQueen.

Even if I hadn't been playing keep-away with my thoughts, I probably would have paid attention to the interview anyway. Tessa was popular in the same way that Perfect Tyler was. Sure, she was pretty in a Disney Channel protagonist way, with her long wavy hair, smooth brown skin sprinkled with a dusting of freckles, and movie-star smile. But she was also super nice and good at what she did.

In my experience, official class politics were much less important than what was going on in the underground, but Tessa was a rare class politician who made her position count. She was a legacy candidate—VP to her older sister, Regina McQueen, as a seventh grader before easily clinching the prez spot once Regina graduated. One of her big initiatives had been the holiday canned-food fundraiser and the carnival it was attached to.

I'd voted for her. It was easy for me to sense competence and passion, and it was clear to me a month in at the Fitz that she had both.

Sitting next to her, slightly out of frame, was Paige Tran, her vice president. Except most people didn't call her

Paige, since there was already a Paige Matthews, who was on the softball team. Most people called her Tractor Tran 'cause, apparently, on the first day of sixth grade, her dad's car had broken down, so he'd dropped her off in the family farm's tractor. Either the nickname didn't bother her or she'd decided to embrace it, because she looked very much the farm girl every time I saw her, including on air that day. Short, no-fuss black hair, overalls, brown somehow-tanned skin even though it was the middle of winter.

She always looked a bit out of place next to Tessa, but they were good friends. Had been since kindergarten, according to Paige's speeches on the campaign trail. But where Tessa was known for being smart and pretty and popular, Paige was known for being Tessa's friend. Well, that and the tractor thing.

"Here with a special announcement about the winter formal, we have student body president Tessa McQueen and VP Paige Tran," Lacey said. "Tessa?"

Tessa flashed a perfect smile. "Thanks, Lacey. I know we were all disappointed about the dance and carnival getting postponed, but we've just taken that opportunity to make both events even more special than before! I talked to Sugar and Spice—the bakery—about donating twenty boxes of doughnuts for the carnival and a chocolate fountain for the dance. And remember, there's going to be a super-secret surprise at the carnival, so be on the lookout for that!"

I wanted to tune out all the dance talk, but I forced myself to keep paying attention as Lacey said, "That all sounds fun. Anything else?"

They sat in silence for three seconds before Tessa gently elbowed Paige, who was still halfway out of frame. She jumped slightly. "Oh, and tickets are still on sale if you haven't already gotten them. You can talk to your homeroom teacher about it."

And I know she wasn't actually looking at me when she said that, but boy did it feel like she was.

The next three classes went by pretty quickly, and all the makeup work was a good distraction. By lunch, I was just about ready to give up the Malik mystery. I'd said we were on a break—and besides, I loved putting together puzzle pieces, but you couldn't do much with just one piece. Even I knew that.

When I told Conor, he seemed surprised.

"Are you sure? Like, I'm not saying you're wrong, but you usually don't let things go like this."

"I can change," I said, biting into my pizza slice with a little too much force.

"Never said you couldn't, dude," Conor shot back before changing the subject.

After lunch was English. Right before the break, we'd just finished reading the survival story *Hatchet*, and now Mr. Yang was having us write reports on it. It was a partner project, which usually meant I'd be doing all the work, but I'd gotten paired with Kennedy Cruz, who I knew would pull her weight. She was a straight A student, our rep for the county spelling bee, and she answered so many questions in class that I was pretty sure I could recognize her from the back of her hand alone.

When we pushed our desks together, she took charge before I could even say anything.

"I think a lot of people are just going to write it like a book report," she said as she set up her water bottle, pencil case, and notebook at perfect right angles on her desk. "We can do better. Like, maybe we can pretend we interviewed the main character and make up quotes that he said?"

I'd had a similar idea—which was a good thing, because she'd phrased it like a question, but I could tell her mind was already made up. "I'm down. I'll come up with questions a reporter would ask, and then we can work on the answers together to make sure they sound like the main character."

"Great," she said. "You can also be in charge of the graphics. In the meantime, I'll start planning the structure and layout. We can maybe take twenty minutes, then swap and check each other's work so far to make sure we're on track?"

"Sounds good."

I skimmed the book for things that would make good interview questions and took notes. Three questions in, the blue of my pen started to fade into faint streaky lines. I shook the pen and tried again. Nothing.

My pockets were a bust, and my backpack seemed to be filled with everything except for a single thing I could use to put words on a piece of paper. I sighed and turned to Kennedy.

"Hey, can I borrow a pen? Mine ran out of ink."

"Yeah, sure," she said, handing me her pencil case without looking up from her work. At this rate, we were going to finish way before the end of the week, when it was due. I wanted to be partnered with Kennedy on everything from now on.

The inside of the pencil case looked like a fully stocked office-supply shop, just like I would have guessed. A variety of highlighters, pens, and perfectly sharpened pencils for all your overachiever needs. I wasn't as picky as she clearly was, so I just grabbed the first pen I saw and started to zip the case back up—but then I stopped.

There's a feeling you get when you know something before you know it. Like when you feel that weird ping at the back of your neck and you turn around and someone is staring at you. The thing that helped keep people alive in caveman times.

I felt it as I spotted something in the pencil case. A single thing out of place: a broken pencil half among the otherwise pristine writing supplies.

And printed right below the eraser? NO. 1.

CHAPTER SIX
MISSING LINK

If there was ever a time in my life for jumpy insides, calm outsides, it was now.

I rezipped the pencil case and put it back on Kennedy's desk, casual as ever. Then I slipped my hand into my pocket, unlocked my phone without taking it out, and just barely slid it out so I could dial the first number on my contact list.

"DJ," said Mr. Yang with his eagle eyes from across the room. "No phones!"

"Sorry, Mr. Yang." I canceled the call and went back to the assignment, completely on autopilot. I hadn't cared too much about the assignment before, besides keeping my grades up, but now, my brain was fully gone. I'd thought I was done with the note that had somehow found its way into my locker, but clearly the hole I'd buried that train of thought into wasn't that deep. The smallest clue and I was spiraling again. But the fact that the clue was small didn't mean it didn't stand for something big. One speck of glitter is small, but there's no such thing as *one* speck of glitter. The stuff gets everywhere once it's out of the shaker.

It was a pencil in a pencil case—not very suspicious by itself. But it was also a broken pencil in a pencil case full of perfect pencils. And it was a number one pencil! I'd never even heard about a number one pencil a week ago, and now I was seeing my second one? And broken in the same way? That didn't feel like a coincidence. That felt like a—

The classroom door suddenly opened. It was Lily, one of the junior peer counselors. Even though they were called peer *counselors*, when things were slow, they also ran errands like the Space Cadets, especially the junior ones.

"Hi, Mr. Yang," she said. "Message for Darius James?"

He pointed me out, and Lily dropped the envelope on my desk. I opened it up to make sure it was what I'd been expecting. It was a hall pass, one I gave to Mrs. Romero at the top of my next class—fifth period Spanish.

She squinted at it confused. "You didn't mention you had a peer-counseling appointment today."

I shrugged apologetically. "I had a mediation earlier in the week, but it ran long. We had to have a second appointment. Sorry it's so last minute."

She handed it back and put a reassuring hand on my shoulder. "Don't be. It's always good to talk through your problems."

Which technically was what I was going to go do. Technically.

I rushed toward the peer counselors' room as fast as I could without actually running, and I was about halfway there when I heard a sharp voice bark, "Hey, no running!"

I groaned and slowed down. It was Caro again. When I looked up, I saw she was with another Space Cadet—Santiago Williams. He was holding a small stack of red flyers with the words JOIN THE SPACE CADETS written in big letters. And he was wearing an expression that would instantly cure me of wanting to do that.

"Come on, Caro," he said, raking his free hand through his mop of black curls. "He wasn't even going that fast."

"Both feet were off the ground at the same time," she said like she was quoting from some manual I knew didn't exist. "That's running."

I didn't think that arguing would get me anywhere I wanted to be, so I just said, "My bad," and showed my hall pass as Santiago flashed me a sympathetic look.

By the time I got to the peer counselors' room, everyone was already there. David met me at the door and led me past Mr. Dyson—who was doing sudoku—and into the back mediation room, where Conor, Audrey, and Monty were posted up.

I clapped David on the shoulder. "Thanks for taking care of getting us the room. And the hall passes for me and the guys." Audrey had the last lunch period, so she'd just needed to walk out once David sent a runner for her.

"Yeah, of course," he said. "Is something wrong? You said you wouldn't call like that unless—" He hesitated. "Actually, I'm just going to sit over there with my headphones on and the volume up as loud as it can go without causing permanent damage to my eardrums."

"Probably for the best," I said. "Conor, watch the window and let him know if anyone is about to walk in." People were supposed to knock first since it was private mediation and confidential, but it couldn't hurt.

Conor nodded. "Sure. But what's going on? Not that

I'm complaining about getting out of math but—"

"Remember the note from yesterday? The BPS one?"

Audrey frowned. "What note?"

"Can we tell them now?" Conor asked.

Audrey's frown deepened. "'Now?' Have you been secretly working this whole time?"

"No! I mean, not really."

She stared at me.

"OK, yes, a little bit. But I didn't go looking for trouble. It just sorta found me."

I filled them in, glossing over the Malik stuff as much as I could without it being enough for Conor to call me out. Eventually, I got to today.

"Last period," I said, "I opened Kennedy's pencil case and boom. Half a number one pencil. Just like this one." I held up the pencil half for them to see. "I know it doesn't seem like much but—"

The frown on Audrey's face softened into more of a confused line, and she shook her head. "No, you're right. That's weird. One time I saw her ask for another Scantron because she colored a tiny bit outside one of the bubbles and couldn't erase it as well as she wanted. She wouldn't keep a half-broken pencil in her pencil case without a good reason."

"Does she have any connection to your friend from your old school?" Monty asked.

"He's not really my friend. And no, not that I know of. I don't believe in coincidences, but I think I have to put that on the back burner for now 'cause I don't really see how it's related to this."

He pointed to the pencil I was holding. "And what about this?"

"Not much of a lead, I know. But this feels . . . it feels bigger than just this. I mean, if you know who I am and what I do, why not just talk to me? An anonymous note, and so vague. Either this person has a flair for the dramatic or they're scared about talking too much."

Audrey looked skeptical.

"What's up, Audrey?" I asked.

"If you think something is going on, I trust you," she said, "but it's hard to imagine anyone being scared of Kennedy."

"You probably know more about her than us," I said. "You're the only non-transfer. Anything we should know?"

She bit her lip in thought. "I mean, I've known her since

elementary school, but we're not friends or anything. She's smart—you have class with her, so you probably know that already. But she doesn't give off big bad mastermind vibes like you or Lucky."

I frowned. "You think I'm threatening?"

"Not to anyone who doesn't deserve it," she said with a grin.

"Well, maybe it's not just her," Conor said. "Maybe she has a crew, and she's the Brains but not the leader?"

"Possible," I said. In my experience, the Brains of the operation also tended to run the group, but not always. "Either way, she's the only lead we have. We should do a deep dive on her. Conor, can you check her socials for anything fishy?"

"Already on it," he said, swiping away at his phone.

"We should also check the school website. Audrey, look for anything that might be BPS related. A person or a club maybe? Anything with those initials. And, Monty, check for anywhere she was mentioned." I held up the snapped pencil that I'd detached from the note. "Meanwhile, I'm going to try and figure this guy out."

I already knew from my research sesh with Conor what

made a number one pencil different from a number two pencil. It wasn't about one being better than the other. Number one pencils just had leads that were softer and made darker marks. They weren't super common, but it wasn't like you had to get them from one super special person we could track down and question. Like everything else, you could just get them online.

The pencil in Kennedy's pencil case had been snapped in half, just like the one in my locker, at about the same length, too. It hadn't been sharpened down like some of the other pencils; it was snapped—and on purpose was my guess. Nothing about the contents of that pencil case had seemed an accident. The collection of supplies and stationery was dripping with precision and forethought, which made the broken pencil seem out of place, even though a pencil case was probably the most logical place for it to be. It was suspicious in its lack of suspiciousness, like it was placed where it wouldn't be questioned.

But why would anyone question a pencil in the first place? I wouldn't, if not for the one I'd been left.

"Found something," said Monty. "It says she's going to the spelling bee in February."

"Oh yeah, I knew that," said Conor.

"You pay attention to the spelling bee?" Audrey asked, sounding like he'd just admitted to bathing in mac and cheese.

"I do when I bet on it," he said. "I lost, like, a thousand tickets on that. Everyone said easy money was on Dominic, but he choked. Two-year streak down the drain."

"OK, back on brand for Conor," Audrey said, giving him a playful punch on the arm.

We researched until our "session" was over, but nothing much turned up.

Audrey found announcements about a "ballet practice session," and I read an article on Wikipedia about the British Pteridological Society (protip: skip it unless you're really into ferns), but neither were helpful.

Conor's social media sweep was similarly unhelpful.

"There's not much there," he said. "Most of it you can only see if you're friends with her, which isn't suspicious so much as smart, and we know that she's smart. There's just enough there to have a presence." As he said that, he flipped through the couple of tame pictures that were viewable by anyone: a younger her in a fluffy dress holding a piece of paper with a red ribbon on it, a more recent picture with her and a friend at the beach, and a really recent one of her onstage having just clinched the spelling bee win. "I can do some more poking around later, but she seems pretty clean."

"Annoying but not a deal-breaker. We just need to get some more information. Do any of you have classes with her?"

"You want us to tail her?" Audrey guessed.

I nodded. "If she has something to do with whatever this is, she'll let on eventually. I mean, why would she be carrying around that pencil if not? It's gotta be driving her crazy. I saw her make sure her notebook was at a right angle to her desk. She wouldn't keep that broken pencil with her unless she needed it for something. What do we know about her schedule?"

"I've seen her walking into art before fifth," Monty said.

"Do you have a class near there?" I asked.

He shook his head. "I was walking to the office. I'm not usually there."

"Hmm," said Audrey thoughtfully. "My fifth-period class is on the other side of school, but if I really book it and sweet-talk Mr. Alderman at the top of next class, then—"

"Nah," I said. "Conor should do it."

"What?" she said. "Why? He's not any closer than me. He has science with Ms. Keyes. That's just as far."

"Yeah, but his tardy record is already totally shot," I said. "One more isn't gonna hurt. Yours is still clean."

"I won't get a tardy," she said. "I can talk my way out of it. I always do."

"Ehh, no reason to risk it," I said. "Caro and the other Space Cadets have been extra harsh lately. Plus, Conor has a lot of experience with tails."

"Trust me, Auds," Conor said, "you're not missing anything."

"I guess," she said, "but when we figure out the rest of her schedule, I wanna help."

"Sure, if she has any classes near yours."

Audrey looked like she was about to say something in response but instead pressed her lips together and made her face blank. As the number one advocate of a good poker face, I knew when I was getting one, and I didn't like it. But I also knew I wasn't going to break hers if she didn't want me to, so I made a note to come back to that and kept going.

"Conor, you check that today, and everyone else, do what you can to figure out the rest of her schedule. Once we know it, we can assign shifts to keep an eye on her between classes. Sound good?"

Everyone agreed that it did, and soon we were out of time and heading back to our next classes.

I'd hoped to clean this up quietly without getting everyone involved, but my gut said this was more than a two-man job, and listening to gut feelings had gotten me out of more than a few scrapes, so I felt like I had to listen. Everyone was on board. It was a real job now.

"OK, Kennedy or Malik or whoever you are," I said under my breath as I walked into the hall. "Game on."

CHAPTER SEVEN
PROTECT AND SERVE

Between the four of us and our connections, we were able to get a pretty good picture of what Kennedy's schedule was like. Conor's snooping on that first day hadn't resulted in anything (besides yet another tardy to his record), but I was sure that if we followed her long enough, something would turn up. And I was right.

The very next day, right in the middle of Conor trying to see how many chicken nuggets he could fit into his mouth (the answer of course being what can only be scientifically described as a disgusting amount), Monty ran up behind him, out of breath, and said, "Hair! Curly hair!"

Conor jumped, and half the contents of his mouth flew out and spattered across the table. None of it got on my lunch tray, but I pushed it away anyway.

"Geez," Conor said, coughing up bits of breading.

"Where did you come from? Are you trying to give a guy a heart attack?"

"Sorry," Monty said, dropping down to sit next to him and speaking through panted breaths, "but I can't forget! I just saw it! It's a guy. Kinda tan skin? Really curly hair. Kinda short—shorter than Audrey."

"Whoa, whoa, slow down. Breathe," Conor said, putting his hands on Monty's shoulders. "What happened? Who are you talking about?"

"I was . . . phew . . . I was on my way back from the bathroom, but then I saw her!"

"Kennedy?" I asked, even though there really wasn't any other *her* he could be talking about.

"Yeah, her! I saw her and that boy, and she opened her pencil case and showed him something, and then he nodded and gave her a little piece of paper, but I don't know who he was, and I don't wanna forget. Uh . . . oh! He was wearing a shirt with a—"

Conor turned his phone screen around to show a text chain with Audrey. He'd already been texting her the description, and she'd come back with an answer attached to a picture.

"Was it him?" Conor asked.

"Yes!" he said, holding out his hand for a high five. "Teamwork!"

I frowned as Conor slapped Monty's hand. "You texted Audrey? She's in class. You're gonna get her in trouble."

"Dude, relax," Conor said. "Monty is also supposed to be in class right now, and you're not worried about him."

"The three of us have priors. Audrey doesn't. We need to keep her clean."

Conor rolled his eyes and sent a text. The response came back fast, and he snorted.

"What?" I asked.

"Nothing," he said, visibly clearing his chat history.

I took a breath. "Well, since you're already unnecessarily bothering her in class, who is he? What do we know about him?"

"His name is Duncan Green," Conor said. "Audrey says he's one of the band geeks. Here, I can pull up his socials." He made a few quick swipes on his phone and then laid it out in the middle of the table so that we all could see. His profiles were a lot more unlocked than Kennedy's had been. We could see a lot more pics, but they were all pretty similar—him in the band room messing around with other band kids.

"Is he friends with Kennedy?" I asked. "Or Audrey? I mean, she recognized him."

"No on Kennedy, at least online," Conor said. "And lemme ask Auds."

I opened my mouth to tell him it could wait, but the message was out before my breath was in.

A few seconds later, he shook his head. "No, she barely knows him. But do you remember the winter concert last year?"

Of course I did. It had happened right before everything had been snowed out, and we'd all gone to watch Audrey. It was a joint choir/orchestra show, and she'd gotten the solo in "O Holy Night," which she'd obviously killed.

"That's how she knows him. He was second tuba." Conor's phone pinged. "No, wait, he's actually first tuba. Good for him I guess?"

"Hmm," I said, pushing food around my tray like one of those Zen gardens because I for sure wasn't eating any of it now. "Band geeks are kind of insular. They stick together.

Mostly just hang out with other band kids. And Kennedy has a couple of friends, but she doesn't cast a really wide net. So, unless it was about homework, I don't know why they'd be talking."

"Yeah, and who goes around showing people their pencil cases?" Conor added. "It's gotta be related."

"I think you're right," I said. "So now we have to figure out, what do these two people have in common? What connects Kennedy Cruz and Duncan Green?"

"They're not in the same grade," Conor pointed out. "She's in seventh; he's in eighth."

"Maybe a homework thing since she's so smart?" Monty suggested.

I made a face. "We can check in with Audrey—*between classes*—but I kinda doubt it."

The most recent picture on Duncan's feed was of him with a pair of drumsticks stuck up his nose. I wasn't really getting diligent-student vibes.

"Hmm, I need to draw this out." I grabbed a notebook from my backpack and made two columns: one for Kennedy, one for Duncan. I didn't like leaving a trail, but we could shred this later. I needed to gather my thoughts.

There was a connection here somewhere. I just needed to find it.

"OK, so Kennedy: Super smart. Seventh grade. Very driven. Spelling bee champ. Duncan: Eighth grade. Band geek. Tuba player. Not super serious."

"Getting anything?" Conor asked.

"Nothing yet," I said. "We're gonna need more info. And, Monty, you need to get back to class before you're missed. But good looking out."

He got up happily and Conor cast a look at my untouched lunch tray.

"Are you gonna—"

"Have a party."

Conor unhinged his jaw to start gulping down my chicken nuggets, which I took as my cue to get a pass to leave lunch early and head to my locker. The halls were always packed after lunch, and I needed to swap my textbooks, but I didn't want to be late for English. If anything happened with Kennedy, I needed to be there to see it. When I got to my locker, the halls were empty, as planned. Well, empty except for one person.

"Audrey!" I hissed, quickly scoping out the hall to

make sure we were alone. I rushed up and pulled her into a corner. "What are you doing here?"

"Aww." She pouted. "I thought I'd be fast enough to get in and out before you got here. I wanted to return the favor."

"What are you talking about?" I asked.

She produced a sour apple lollipop from her pocket. "I won this in class for getting a hundred on my last quiz. I was gonna put it in your locker."

"Congrats on the quiz, but you could have given me this after class. We've talked about this, Audrey. It's dangerous."

She scoffed playfully. "Oh, like me texting in class?"

"Yes! And class isn't out yet. This is a risk for no reason."

Her eyes set just a bit, not angry exactly but... annoyed? Is that what I'd sensed before but couldn't quite place?

"First of all," she said, "I texted in class before I met you, and it always turned out fine, so don't act like I'm taking some big risk by doing something pretty much everyone in school does, including the teachers. And second of all, it wasn't a risk for no reason. It was a risk because I wanted to do something nice for you." She stuck out the lollipop pointedly, and I wasn't sure if I should take it.

"Audrey, I—"

"Hey," said a voice from behind us. I turned and saw the shiny, star-shaped badge of a Space Cadet glinting in the fluorescent light attached to one Santiago Williams. I kicked myself. We were in a corner, but we were still in the middle of the hall. You *never* talk out in the open like this. And I was the one who'd been talking about unnecessary risks.

"Do you two have hall passes?" he asked.

I started opening my mouth to cover for Audrey, but before I could, Audrey said with a cheery smile, "Oh, Santiago, there you are!"

"Huh?" he said, which is what I was thinking.

She offered him the lollipop she'd just offered me. "Candygram! From an anonymous sender." She added that last part in a teasing whisper, like it was a secret.

"Oh, wow. Really?" He took the lollipop, the tips of his ears starting to turn red. "I didn't even know the school did candygrams."

She shrugged. "Hey, I just deliver them. But enjoy!" She flashed a smile and then disappeared down the hall, leaving Santiago staring at the lollipop in his hands. Then he seemed to remember I was standing there.

"Oh, hall pass?" I produced the one I'd gotten earlier, and he nodded and left me alone. Internally, I breathed a sigh of relief. What had I been thinking? Trying to bail Audrey out? She bailed other people out. That was her whole thing. I'd almost screwed up things for both of us. And what if it had been Caro instead of Santiago? Or someone like Mr. Kind? We had no idea how long this tailing mission would last. It wasn't a set number of risks we were taking; they were gonna be long-term and sustained. Plenty of opportunity for something to go wrong.

We needed a better system. We needed access.

I looked up and saw Santiago walking away from me, shiny badge giving him access to the halls during class time, no questions asked.

We needed that.

CHAPTER EIGHT
SPACE RACE

When I laid out the Space Cadet HELP WANTED poster in front of the team after school at Audrey's place, Conor laughed for about thirty seconds straight.

"The Space Cadets?" he said, struggling to catch his breath. "You want us to join the Space Cadets?"

"It doesn't have to be all of us," I said. "But it would be nice to have one person with a little extra freedom of movement. Plus, Space Cadets have access to places other kids don't, like the front office and stuff. It's a good asset long term."

Conor snorted. "Well, count me out. I wouldn't wear that stupid badge for all the tickets we scored last year."

"Shocker," I said. "That leaves the three of us, and Audrey—"

"It should be Monty," Audrey said, shutting down anything else I had to say. "He's big, he's tough-looking, and if you give me a comb and some hair gel, I can make him look like G.I. Joe. You see how Caro runs the cadets. She thinks it's like an actual military operation. The teacher is technically in charge of who gets in, but Caro steamrolls everyone she talks to, including adults. It's her pick, and she'll snap him up right away."

"That's . . . basically what I was gonna say."

She gave a mock bow.

"You could take over my job."

"Well, I might if you won't let me do mine," she said . . . jokingly? She didn't look annoyed like she had before, but she was literally our Face. She could look like anything she wanted. But she wouldn't be mad at me and not tell me . . . right? Her playful eyes almost seemed to dare me to ask her, but I honestly wasn't prepared for the answer, so I just coughed awkwardly.

"Um, right. I was thinking we'd look into Caro's socials. See what she's into and memorize it so you can get on her good side."

"Are you sure I can do this?" Monty asked.

"Aww, Monty." Audrey smoothed out his hair. "You'll be great. I promise. Here. Come with me to the bathroom, and we'll see what we can do with your hair. Oh, and I can raid my dad's closet for some clothes that make you look more Caro approved. You can go over her social media profiles while I'm doing that."

"I can—" I started, but Audrey cut me off again.

"Don't worry, I can handle this. You and Conor should see if there's any connection between Kennedy and Duncan. You were right, it *is* weird for them to be hanging out. She's so into school, and he doesn't care about any of his classes except for band. He really gets in the zone when he's playing. I was, like, right across from him during the concert, so I could see how much he was concentrating."

"And she has no band connection?" Conor asked.

"I don't think so," Audrey said. "But I'll tell you if I remember something. Come on, Monty!"

She walked off, Monty in tow, and I watched her leave before turning to Conor.

"So," I asked. "Were you getting a vibe or—?"

"Oh, there's definitely a vibe," Conor said. "You're in trouble," he singsonged.

"What? Why? Did she say something?"

"What's that thing you're always saying about lips and ships and sinking?"

I swatted him with a pillow. "Did she say something or not?"

"Man, for such a smart kid you are *dumb*, DJ. Do you know that?"

"What's *that* supposed to mean?"

"I'm saying," he said, smacking me back with the pillow, "that it's pretty obvious that she's mad at you because you didn't ask her out to the dance before."

I made a face. "That's not it."

"Do you have a better theory?"

I thought I might, but I didn't really want to think about it, so I kept my mouth shut, which Conor took as a win.

"I'm telling you," he said. "You can make this go away for the low, low price of some dance tickets and one of those wrist flower thingies."

I didn't think he was right, but that didn't stop me from feeling bad about it.

Conor and I did our best to find a connection between Kennedy and Duncan, but twenty minutes later, we were still no closer to figuring it out. Audrey, on the other hand, had had much more success.

She came out of the bathroom, holding up a hairbrush like a mic and putting on her best announcer voice. "He's serious. He's polite. He's got so much gel in his hair it's ridiculous. Introducing the new and Caro-approved Montgomery LaCroix."

At his cue, Monty walked out, hair smartly slicked down, military jacket and tee swapped out for a polo shirt, and jeans swapped for crisp khakis. Forget Space Cadets, he looked like he might be an actual cop.

"Oh man, I hate this," Conor said. "Meaning Caro is gonna love it. Good job, you guys."

"Thanks," Monty said, moving to touch his hair.

Audrey swatted at his hand, and he dropped it back to his side. "I hope this works."

"Nah, man, you're gonna crush it," Conor said. "Think about it. How many applications do you think they're actually gonna get? Caro is the worst."

"He's right," I said. "Not about Caro being the worst."

"She is."

"About there not being very many applications. Space

Cadets isn't the most popular group. Most kids think they're annoying. This is less about getting the job and more about getting on Caro's good side. She's the one who chooses patrol assignments. I have a plan, and if it's gonna work, you need to get the one that you want."

"You're not gonna be able to wear an earpiece," Audrey said. "If she sees you using tech in school you won't get it. She's a total stickler for the rules. And if you hide it with a hat or something it will ruin the look. But don't worry; you got this."

"Besides," Conor said. "She's a classic petty tyrant. All you gotta do is agree with her on everything and she'll like you."

"He's right," I said again. "He refuses to get along with her, but he's right."

"I have principles," Conor said, tossing his hair dramatically and making Audrey giggle.

She seemed like she was in a good mood. I didn't want to disrupt that. Knowing when to leave well enough alone is important—but knowing when to check the room for a ticking bomb is, too.

The flyers said that interviews for Space Cadets were

before school, during lunch, and after school. We planned to get Monty to school early. If he could get badged up that same day, we had a chance to try something before the week was up and we'd have to wait a whole weekend for access to our main suspects.

Monty arranged to get an early ride to school from his brother, with Audrey tagging along mostly for moral support but also to do damage control if necessary. Then, we walked through possible options for the next day until Monty's brother came to pick him up. Conor's sister showed up a few minutes later. While Conor went to her car, I hung back for a sec.

"Hey, Audrey."

She stopped, having been about to close the door. "Hmm? Did you forget something?"

"No, I, uh. Earlier. In the hall. With Santiago."

Her eyes widened a bit, like she was curious about where I was going. That made two of us. Even though I'd been thinking about it as we'd been talking, I still didn't know exactly what I was gonna say. But I'd started, so I had to finish.

"When you gave Santiago your lollipop . . . is that because you were mad at me?"

The corner of her lip quirked up into a dry smile. "No, DJ. I gave it to him because I got caught in the hallway with no hall pass and I needed an excuse to leave."

"OK, good. 'Cause, I would hate it if you were mad at me."

Her face softened, and she put a hand on my shoulder. "I'm not mad at you, DJ. I promise. Now just focus on making sure the Three Little Pigs plan for tomorrow goes off without a hitch."

"Three Blind Mice," I corrected.

She smiled.

"Oh, you know that. You were messing with me."

"Just a little," she admitted. "Now go. Bethany's waiting."

She went to close the door again, and I stopped her one more time.

"Wait."

"What?"

"What were you gonna do if you'd already given me the lollipop?"

And she looked at me like I'd asked her what color the sky was.

"Same as always. Improvise."

CHAPTER NINE
SEE HOW THEY RUN

The next day on the way to school, I got a text from Monty. Three mouse emojis. That was the signal. He was in. The plan was on.

We'd never done a proper Three Blind Mice before, but it wasn't like Moonwalking Bear levels of complicated. It was actually super simple. It didn't have anything about mice or blinding anyone. It was about the next line of the rhyme. You know: "Three Blind Mice, See how they run." We didn't know who Kennedy was working with besides Duncan, but she was a jumpy person. With a little pressure, maybe we could chase her back to her mousehole and take a peek inside.

After lunch was English, and we were still working on our group projects. So once attendance was done, I scooted my desk next to Kennedy and we got to work. I kept one eye on my paper and one eye on the clock. I hadn't gotten a signal otherwise, which meant Monty had a hall-monitoring shift at the end of this period.

Just like before, Kennedy took out her supplies and arranged them on her desk like they were toy soldiers keeping watch. We'd made pretty good progress on our presentation, but we still had plenty left to do. All I had to do was make sure she stayed nice and distracted for most of class, find an excuse to get into her pencil case, and—

"I had some free time between spelling bee practice and math homework last night and I decided to take a break to finish up our project," she said, laying down a completed article in front of me.

Uh-oh.

"You— All of it?"

"Mm-hm. We can turn it in now if we want. I want to ask Mr. Yang if I can go to the library for the rest of the period since we're done."

Oh, this wasn't good. If she was in the library, that threw off our entire plan. I had to keep her here until it was time.

"Hold on," I said. "Let's not rush this. Shouldn't we double-check everything?"

"I did."

"Triple-check, then," I said. "This is a big project. It's gonna affect our GPAs a lot."

Everyone has their trigger words, and *GPA* was clearly one of hers—no big surprise. She struck me as the kind of person who believed the permanent record was a real thing and not just a thing adults made up to scare kids. I could see the doubt creep into her eyes about what I was sure was already an A project. But she wasn't just an A student. She was an A-plus student.

"Do you think that's a good idea?" she asked, without any of the take-charge attitude from the first day.

"For sure," I said. "Here, we can go through line by line."

I'll spare you the excruciating deep dive into our project, but about five minutes before the end of class, we were nearing the end of the paper—and the start of my plan.

"I was really feeling *distressing* for this line, but now I'm thinking *traumatic*? Or *harrowing*? But that might be too dramatic. What do you think?"

"Hmm," I said, pretending to think it over while I eyed her pencil case, which was sitting between our desks. It was zipped shut, but I could change that. "Let me write the sentence out with the other options. See how they look."

I started writing with my pencil but pressed down hard enough to break the lead.

"Ugh," I said. "Do you mind if I—"

Just like before, she handed the pencil case to me without a thought. Whatever else was going on with her, she wasn't stingy with her supplies, I had to give her that.

I zipped open the case and mentally crossed my fingers that she hadn't moved the pencil in the meantime. Nope, there it was, rolling around with its perfectly sharpened neighbors. I grabbed it along with a fresh pencil, hiding the broken one in my palm. Then I knocked the case a little bit farther—closer to the edge of the table.

I glanced at the clock. Four minutes to the bell. Monty should be in range. Time to hook Kennedy. I had the pencil, but that didn't matter if she didn't know that I had it. I stealthily dropped the pencil half into my lap, then grabbed it under the table with my other hand and put it in my pocket.

"OK," I said. "Let's think about this." And, at the same time, I kicked the table, knocking the pencil case off the side.

Pens, pencils, erasers, and a very nice sharpener went clattering across the floor. Kennedy's eyes went wide—wider than they should have for something this annoying but harmless.

She immediately sprang into action, scooping up the items like Easter eggs and putting them into the pouch.

"My bad!" I said. "Let me help."

"No!" she said, her voice weirdly aggressive. "I mean, it's fine. I have it."

That was extreme control freak behavior, even for her. If I hadn't already been sure that we were onto something, I would be now. She carefully combed the classroom floor for her missing supplies, but I knew she wasn't going to find what she was really looking for. She couldn't. I had it.

"Mr. Yang," she said, dropping her case on her desk and picking at her nails. "Can I go to the bathroom?"

"Yeah," he said. "Take the hall pass."

She grabbed the hall pass, walked to the door, and then

walked back, grabbing a pen from her desk. "We can finish this later," she said to me as she rushed out the door.

The "run" part of "see how they run" isn't usually so literal, but it was promising. With Kennedy gone, I waited to make sure no one was looking and then slipped the pencil half back into her pencil case, right at the bottom. Hopefully, she'd see it and write the whole incident off as a case of missing the obvious and paranoia. It happened. Not today, but it happened.

I felt my phone ping two minutes later but waited to check it until the bell rang and I was out of the room. No reason to have Mr. Yang call me out for in-class phone usage twice in one week. If he started really watching me, I'd have a problem.

The second I was out, though, I saw a message from Monty: *Went to locker #243. The one with all the stickers on it near the library. Dropped in a note.*

That explained why she'd needed the pen. But whose locker was that?

Conor texted back before I could say anything: *I have class in that hall next period. I can leave early and scope out if anyone passes by.*

Monty: I have another shift the period after if that doesn't work.

Audrey: And I can cover passing between sixth and seventh.

I grinned. My team, on top of it as usual.

Conor ended up getting back to us with news first. *Got her,* he texted, followed by a picture of a girl pulling books from the locker. She was short with bright red hair and a bulging backpack.

Audrey: *That's Jenna Tucker. Art kid.*

That's where I'd recognized her from. There'd been a countywide art contest for Thanksgiving, and she was the winner from our school, so she'd gotten a piece of her art displayed in city hall along with the other winners.

So now we had a nerd, a band geek, and an art kid. Still no obvious connection.

Does she hang out with the others? I asked.

Audrey: *Don't think so.*

Conor: *I'll check her socials.*

Figure out what you can. We'll regroup after school. I stowed my phone and walked into my next class, Spanish.

The room was dark when I walked in, which meant we were watching a movie. Whenever Mrs. Romero didn't feel like making us conjugate verbs or stumble through awkward conversations in broken Spanish, she'd throw on the Spanish version of a Disney movie. I wasn't sure how helpful it was to us actually learning anything, but I wasn't about to complain—and teachers need breaks, too.

I was a little curious about what "Hakuna Matata" sounded like in Spanish, but as soon as the movie was on, my mind went right back to our new piece of information.

Jenna Tucker. Art kid.

Was she the ringleader? Pencils could be an art thing. But pretty much everyone in the building had to use pencils for something or another. It would be serious jumping to conclusions to assume one had something to do with the other.

What else did I know about her? Not much. Conor was checking her socials. All I knew was that she'd won that art contest. Kennedy had made me do the art parts for our assignment, so it didn't seem like she was into art. And Duncan basically only posted about band stuff.

It wasn't that different people couldn't work together.

The gang and I were all pretty different, and we worked together great. But there had to be some common thread. Something to connect a contest-winning artist, a spelling bee champ, and the second-chair tuba.

First chair, I mentally corrected myself. Audrey had sent that follow-up text. He'd been promoted to first chair. That meant he wasn't the second-best tuba player in school anymore, he was number one.

Wait.

Number one. Like the pencil half that was stashed in my backpack at all times for safekeeping. *Number one.* I felt my brain seize on the words like a dog playing tug-of-war. There was something there; I could feel it. But what was on the other side of the rope I was pulling?

If it was about being the best, being number one, then they all fit there. They'd all just won things or ranked up. But so what? Why would someone send me a coded message about that?

I thought back to the info we'd gathered on Duncan and Kennedy. The dozens of goofy pics of Duncan with his band friends. The few sparse pics of Kennedy—her at the beach, her at the bee, her with a ribbon.

A red ribbon.

A red second-place ribbon.

I felt my hand shoot into the air, almost before I realized what I was doing. "¿Puedo ir al baño?" I blurted out. As soon as I had the hall pass, I was out the door and beelining for the nearest bathroom. I had a theory. A big, wild, crazy theory. But it was a grounded kind of crazy. A crazy-enough-to-be-true kind of crazy.

Kennedy hadn't been the favorite to win the spelling bee. That's what Conor had said before: *"I lost, like, a thousand tickets on that. Easy money was on Dominic, but he choked. Two-year streak down the drain."*

And I didn't know about what had gone on with Duncan and his band-placement test, but Audrey had gotten it wrong the first time. She'd said he was second chair and then corrected herself. Was it a simple mistake? Or a recent development? And then there was Jenna.

I got behind the safety of a stall door and whipped out my phone, typing in *Jenna Tucker art contest* and hitting search. An article from the local paper popped up about the Thankful Thoughts art contest.

Thankful Thoughts. That was the name of the contest.

I searched for that on our school website. There was an announcement from late November listing Jenna as the winner from our school, along with the runners-up.

Under that was an announcement from the year before listing the winner—Martina Breyer—and second place—Jenna Tucker. And the year before that? Martina Breyer winner and Jenna Tucker second.

I could feel my hands shaking. I held on to my phone tighter so I wouldn't accidentally drop it into the toilet. A picture was forming in my mind. I didn't have it all yet, but it was like when you almost finish the border pieces of a puzzle. There was just one more corner piece I needed to slot in. I texted Audrey.

Me: *Did anything weird happen during Duncan's band placement test?*

Audrey: *What happened to no texting during school? Kidding. I'll find out.*

I slipped my phone back into my pocket, flushed the toilet out of habit, and made myself stop vibrating. There was no way I could play it off that I was that excited to watch *The Lion King* for the millionth time.

I never wanted Audrey to text me in the middle of class

more in my life, and I got my wish during the second half of seventh-period history. I felt my phone buzz and hid it behind my textbook as I checked it out.

Audrey: *Jade Collins was first tuba before Duncan. My friend in band said she lost the spot because, on test day, she misplaced her tuba. Didn't find it until today. Wild, right? How do you misplace a tuba?*

You don't, I thought as I slotted the last puzzle piece in. *You absolutely don't.*

I needed to talk to the others.

CHAPTER TEN
THE TIP OF THE ICEBERG

As soon as class was over, I texted Conor: *Don't wait for me. Go straight to Audrey's. I'll be there as soon as I can.* I had to make a quick stop, and I wanted to make sure the gang was ready to go as soon as I burst through the door—and I mean that very literally. You don't always get to do dramatic entrances, and they're unnecessary, but even I have to admit they're really exciting.

"It's a setup!" I said, barreling through Audrey's front door as Monty opened it for me.

Conor and Audrey were already sitting up on the couch, looking a little lost.

"What's going on, DJ?" Audrey asked.

"Yeah," added Conor. "Texting her in class. Sending me straight here?"

"I got it," I said. "I know what it is. The BPS. Think

about it. Kennedy. Duncan. Jenna. What do they all have in common?"

"Nothing?" Conor said with a shrug. "I checked out Jenna's stuff like you said. She's not friends with either of them, and all she posts is art stuff."

"Wrong," I said. "They do have something in common. One big thing." I pulled out a pencil, a regular number two pencil. "Number two. Kennedy? She was supposed to lose the spelling bee to Dominic. That's what you said."

"But he choked," Conor filled in. "He was all jumpy, like it was his first time."

"Yeah, super weird from a two-time champ. And Duncan? He was second-chair tuba until last placement test, right, Audrey?"

"Yeah," she said. "That's what my band friend said. Until Jade misplaced her tuba."

"How do you misplace a tuba?" asked Monty.

Conor snorted. "Right? It's like the size of a full kid."

"Exactly!" I said. "And on the day of your big test? There's no way."

"Jenna won the art contest," Monty said, catching on. "Was she not supposed to?"

"She always comes in second place," I said. "The past two years she came in second place to the same girl. Martina Breyer. I just came from the art room and asked if Martina entered. She couldn't. She made a clay pot, but someone accidentally knocked it over after school and it shattered."

"And by accidentally you mean—"

"*Accidentally,*" I said, completing Audrey's sentence with the most aggressive air quotes I could. "That's what the BPS is. They're the number two kids sabotaging the kids on top to take their places."

"Whoa," said Conor. "That's like some serious Illuminati stuff."

"I know," I said. "But we know something is going on. And three different switchovers so close together? It can't be a coincidence. They've gotta be helping each other. Jenna can't risk breaking the pot herself, but if someone else does it, it looks like an accident. And I bet Kennedy helped hide that tuba. Maybe that piece of paper he gave her had something to do with the tuba heist?"

"I didn't say I didn't believe you," Conor said. "I'm just sayin', if this is what's going on, it could be massive, dude."

"I think it has to be," I said. "'Cause I was thinking. About the pencils. Like, why use them?"

"Didn't you already get that?" Conor said. "I mean, assuming you're right. Number one, number two, right?"

"I mean, yeah," I said. "Whoever is doing this obviously has a flair for the dramatic with the whole symbolic-pencil thing. But that's not what I mean." I turned to Monty. "You saw Kennedy show Duncan her pencil before he handed her that piece of paper, right?"

"I only saw the case, but I'd bet anything it was the pencil she was showing him," said Monty, nodding.

"So why would you do that?" I asked. "What would showing the pencil prove?"

"You only flash two things like that," said Conor. "A threat or ID. It could have been a threat, but I'm thinking ID."

"Why?"

"Because we got one, too," Audrey guessed correctly.

"Exactly. There's more than these floating around, which makes me think it's a kind of calling card—like a secret handshake or something."

"Also, pencils aren't super threatening," Monty chimed in.

"That too. And think about it. If there are only two people in a conspiracy, there's no reason to have ID. Our group is four, and we don't have any special ID cards. You have to have a certain number of people and be operating with a certain level of secrecy before you need ID like this. The kind of thing where not everyone knows everyone else in the group."

"There's something I don't get," Conor said. "If the pencils are ID, why send one to you? You're not in their little club."

"Maybe they want him to be?" Audrey suggested.

"Possible, but I doubt it," I said. "Remember the note? It was so vague. Why would they just send me three letters and nothing else? No information. No instructions."

"As a test to get in?" Conor offered.

"You really think *Duncan Green* figured all this out by himself?"

"Good point."

"And wasn't the BPS in the note crossed out?" Audrey added. "They probably wouldn't do that in an invitation now that I think about it."

I nodded. "Agreed. My best guess is the note is from

someone who knows what's going on and isn't a fan but is too scared to do anything about it. Which is fair. It seems like the BPS has a lot of people they can sic on anyone who gets in their way."

"How many people?" Monty wondered.

"Conor was right. This really is starting to feel a little Illuminati," said Audrey. "How deep do you think this goes?"

"Well," I said. "It's Friday, which means we have the entire weekend to search. Let's find out."

Once we started looking, the evidence was everywhere. It was like when you learn a word for the first time and then hear it three times the next day. Monty caught the first one.

"I might have something," he said, pausing his phone and getting our attention. "Last basketball game, Colby scored twenty points and he was on the bench before. Second string."

I remembered hearing about that on the announcements, I just hadn't been paying attention then, or I had but to the wrong thing.

"That definitely could be something," I said, adding it to the list.

Conor came through with the next one.

"Yo, look at this," he said. "Benji replaced Alana as Quiz Bowl captain, which makes no sense. She got them to the finals two years running."

"And I'm gonna assume you know this because—"

"I have bets on them, too. Yes. Obviously."

Audrey swatted me on the shoulder. "Oh! I just thought of something. In choir, Hailey—that's Ariel from the musical—was supposed to have the eighth-grade solo at the winter concert, but she said she felt sick and the director gave it to Cindra at the last minute."

I felt my heartbeat pick up a bit. None of us were really in clubs except for Audrey, and she was great at everything she did. If we were right about what was going on, she'd be a clear target.

"Hey, DJ," she said, snapping me out of it. "I can see what you're thinking. Stop it. I don't think anyone is trying to bump me off."

"Hey, he's right," said Conor. "If they're going after all the best people, then you might have a target on your back."

She chuckled. "That's supersweet, but I'm not the best."

"Yes, you are," Monty said, sounding almost offended that she'd say that.

A thought struck me. "Weren't you just saying the other day that Brent was super salty that you got the seventh-grade solo instead of him?"

Audrey laughed again, but this time it was a bit more uneasy. "Come on. He was a little upset, but that doesn't mean he'd do anything to me."

"He wouldn't have to," I pointed out. "He joins up and boom. Someone else to do his dirty work. All your sheet music is shredded, your water bottle is spiked with hot sauce, and he's singing 'Defying Gravity' at the spring concert instead of you!"

"Come on, DJ. I'm not going to do 'Defying Gravity.' That's too obvious. I'm thinking maybe 'Last Midnight.'"

It was a paper-thin deflection from the best Face I knew. She was barely even trying.

I huffed out a breath. "Audrey. This is serious."

"I know, I know." She rubbed her shoulder with her right hand. "It's just kind of creepy, you know? All this is happening, and if I didn't know you guys, I wouldn't even know I might be mixed up in it."

She was right. It was weird to think about. She could be in just as much danger with no way of knowing. I'd hate that. More than I hated the idea of her getting busted for working on our jobs.

"Well, since you know about this, you can watch your back. We'll help watch it, too, right, guys?"

Conor and Monty chimed in enthusiastically, and she smiled gratefully.

"Thanks, guys. And I'll follow the lead with Hailey. Don't worry, I'll be careful about it."

"I know you will. We should also get a list of all the clubs at school and see if there have been any shake-ups recently. Maybe we can figure out how long this has been going on."

We grabbed a list of clubs and activities from the school website, split them up, and spent the weekend digging. We had to do a lot of cross-referencing—not everything was big enough to make the morning announcements or the school website. But between the announcement transcripts on the AV Club page, celebration posts from recently promoted students, pictures that gave away more than they intended I'm sure, and salty posts from former number ones, a picture began to take shape.

Chess Club, Debate Club, and Quiz Bowl had seen sudden changes in leadership. Choir, the bowling team, and Junior Model UN had seen sudden last-minute swaps. The musical that Audrey and I had been in had needed the understudy to go on for Prince Eric. By the time we were through the list, we had twenty clubs that we thought might be involved, stretching back to September. There was no guarantee that every single one of them was connected, but that was too many for it to mean nothing.

"And you wouldn't notice," I said when we regrouped to talk about our leads on Sunday. "You wouldn't notice because it's spread out across all these different clubs. A lot in the geek block at first—science fair, Quiz Bowl, that kind of thing. Then it branches out. Choir. Band. Basketball."

"Tyler better watch out," Conor said with a snort. "Looks like they finally made their way up to the jocks."

He was joking, but the thought had crossed my mind. It wasn't baseball season yet, but if it was, I'd be worried about him.

"We'll need to properly vet these leads," I said. "This is a lot of information, and we want to make sure we're not chasing shadows. I'm thinking we do some tailing, some subtle questioning. If we can figure out their MO, maybe we can figure out who's behind it. There's gotta be a ringleader. Or maybe a couple. But this is way too many people and clubs for there not to be central leadership. Audrey, I'm gonna need you to take point on the questioning."

"Of course," she said. "I already have some ideas about who I want to talk to first."

"Monty and Conor, I want you two checking up on our suspects. See if they talk to each other. Flash pencils. Things like that."

"Got it, boss," said Conor.

"Report everything back to me. I'll be keeping track of what we find. And if I can help out with the tailing or talking let me know, but—"

Conor clapped a hand on my shoulder. "Don't worry. We got this. You concentrate on making your little conspiracy board."

There was no actual board with pictures and red string, but that was basically my next three days. Throughout the day, my phone would ping with messages from the group:

> *Audrey: Hailey wasn't sick-sick! She got an anonymous note in her locker that Tyler said she was totally stuck-up! Totally BPS shenanigans! Maybe something similar happened with Dominic and the spelling bee to throw him off?*
>
> *Monty: Saw Colby talking to Jenna during passing. His locker isn't anywhere near hers. Suspicious.*
>
> *Conor: Duncan has a pencil!!!! Illuminati confirmed.*

I noted every connection, tracked every name, combed through the list for any sense of hierarchy. Any clear leader. But I didn't find one. Some of them, like Kennedy and Benji, were definitely smart enough to run something like this, but they didn't give me strong mastermind vibes. And I wasn't confident either of them had the charisma to get people on their side. Maybe one of them was the Brains of the operation and they had a Face for recruitment? Anything was possible.

And by the looks on everyone's faces when I laid this out during our post-school meetup on Wednesday, they were feeling that, too.

"Well, that sounds like a lot to unpack sooo . . ." Conor

riffled around in his backpack and proudly pulled out a ziplock bag of neon green powder. "Sugar break!"

Audrey sighed. "Conor."

"What? I didn't even blow that many tickets on them. It was a steal."

"Yeah, because Royce's stuff is terrible! That's probably fifty percent powdered sugar."

He shrugged. "Sugar is sugar, man."

She made a face. "If you're gonna get all hopped up on sugar, couldn't you at least buy from Choi? Doesn't he have the good stuff?"

Conor was already licking up a handful of the dust he'd poured into his hand. "Yeah, but he wasn't at his usual after-school spot, so I had to make do."

"You didn't hear?" said Monty. "Choi was busted."

Conor jumped like he'd been shocked, leaving a dusting of sugar on Audrey's coffee table. "*What?* No!"

This was news to me. I didn't pay the most attention to Choi and his little sugar empire, but he was a major player in the school. And he was careful.

"Santiago told me," Monty said. "There was a report about a broken stall in the bathroom, so he brought the vice principal to come look at it. When they walked in, Choi was caught red-handed selling an entire case of Fun Dip. He's been shut down since Monday."

"Nooooo," Conor said, sinking to the floor dramatically. Then he jolted up violently. "Wait, no!"

"What?" I asked.

"Oh man, we're so stupid!"

"Speak for yourself," said Audrey.

"No, listen! We've just been looking at official clubs. Stuff on the books. But what about the underground? Choi is a top dog. He has been forever. Took over the business from his older brother. Everyone knows he has the good stuff, like you guys said. If the BPS is targeting all the best people at school? Boom, target."

He was right. How had we missed it? Why wouldn't the already shady members of the school be involved in this huge conspiracy? In fact, why wouldn't one of them be *running* it? Career criminals already had a ton of experience sneaking around, dealing with big groups of people, coordinating logistics—contraband sugar, homework forging, tournaments . . .

"Dino Death Match!" I said. "Conor! You're the best!"

"I know," he said. Then he stopped as he caught my meaning. "Oh. *Oh!* Ha! Ambrose *was* cheating! He was cheating with my cheats! I bet he was! I don't know how he got them, but I bet he was! Second best in Lucky's tourney. Second best to me. That's got BPS written all over it."

I shook my head to clear it like an Etch A Sketch. If I was making a physical conspiracy board, I'd need to wheel in a second one for this new info. It seemed like no matter what I did, I couldn't quite escape the school's less noble criminal element. But it was for a good cause. We were getting somewhere.

"OK," I said, already formulating our next moves in my mind. "New plan. I think it's time to get our hands a little dirty."

CHAPTER ELEVEN
WOLF'S CLOTHING

We decided on a two-pronged approach: one aboveground, one below.

"Before we got this new lead, I was gonna suggest we join a club and try to get in closer contact with the BPS people, but now that we think Royce is involved, that changes things."

"Do you want me to talk to him?" Audrey asked.

I shook my head. "No, I want you and Monty to stick to the first plan. Try to find a club to join. Something with hierarchy and structure or opportunities only one person can get. Something they don't have their claws in yet."

"A cappella is about to open auditions," she said. "I was thinking about joining anyway. Monty and I could both sign up."

"Great," I said. "And in the meantime, Conor and I can hit up Royce."

By now, we'd collected a list of people we were pretty sure were BPS members, but we hadn't made contact. The second we asked someone, "Hey, are you a part of this secret society?," we lost our control. There was nothing stopping them from reporting back that we were looking into them. And we saw the things they were willing to do to people standing in their way. I didn't wanna find out what they'd do to us if they realized we were actively working against them.

If we were gonna talk to someone, it had to be someone we knew was sloppy. Someone who maybe didn't care so much about whatever rules this secret society must have. Who wasn't gonna rat us out first thing. Someone like Royce.

"Are you sure you don't want backup?" Audrey asked. "If not me, Monty."

"Nah," I said. "Royce is an idiot. Me and Conor can handle him. That's why he's such a great target. And it will be less suspicious for Conor to be talking to him anyway, since he's already a customer."

"You're not a customer," Conor pointed out.

"Yeah, but someone has to make sure you don't stick your foot in your mouth."

"Hey!" Conor dipped his tongue directly into the bag of sugar. "But fair."

"OK," she said. "As long as you're sure. My advice, though? The best way to get someone to talk to you is to make them think you're one of them. If I walk into a room wearing my *Wicked* T-shirt, I don't have to figure out who the other *Wicked* fans are in the room—they find me. It's like ID to the club."

"You're saying we should bring the pencil," I said, and she nodded.

"If you can make another one for Conor, that would be good, too. I don't know if Royce will ask, but like you said, better safe than sorry."

"My brother's new job is at the mall," Monty chimed in. "They have an art-supply store. I can ask him to get me some number one pencils."

"Yeah," I said. "Definitely ask your brother. Come to school early, and Conor can whip us up a forgery before we see Royce. If you have any problems, let us know."

We did a little bit more coordinating to make sure everyone knew what they were doing, and eventually, we all headed home.

* * *

The next morning, Conor met me in front of the school with the pencils from Monty.

"He and Audrey are doing the a cappella thing," Conor said. "He left the pencils with me."

"Did you make the fake already?" I asked.

"No, but I don't think I have to. Look." He pulled a broken pencil half out of his pocket and held it up to me. It was broken cleanly in the middle like the one that had been left in my locker, and the sharp splintered end had been rubbed down. The paint was chipped, and the sides were scuffed.

"Where did you get this?" I asked. "Did you find it?"

"Nah, Monty made it. It's good, right?" He pointed to the sides. "They were brand-new out of the box, so he roughed it up to make it look like we'd had it for a while. Like the other one we have. See all the little marks? It's like it's been riding around in his pocket for weeks."

"Did you ask him to do this?"

"Nah, but it's good, right? I don't think I would have done anything different. He did this one on his own to try it out and gave me the rest of the pencils in case it didn't work, but I think Monty has a future in forgery. I gotta see what else he can whip up."

I took the pencil from Conor and turned it around in my fingers. It was a broken number one pencil. Not exactly rocket science, but I was still nervous. My cell phone is identical to every other cell phone of the same kind, more or less, but if I picked up the wrong one, I'd still be able to tell almost instantly because of the specific nicks and scratches and the way it feels in my hand. What if this was the same? What if Royce saw through us?

"Hey," Conor said, reading my face. "Don't worry. Royce is an idiot. He probably won't even ask to see these. It's like a backup, right?"

I shook away my fears and gave him back the fake. "Right. And this looks good. I've been thinking about shoring up Monty's soft skills. I might have you work with him here."

"Yeah, sure." He jerked his thumb toward the school's entrance. "Do you wanna handle this now or during lunch?" Conor asked. "Lunch is when I usually see him."

"We should try to find him now, before school starts," I said. "He'll probably be less busy. The fewer people, the better. Do you know where he'd be posted?"

"He usually just hangs out in the halls and sells out of his backpack, but the other day, he was set up in the bathroom in the main hallway. That's Choi's normal spot."

That made sense. Choi's operation was pretty clean, despite where it took place. It was private, easy to flush merch if he had to, and half of his customer base would pass through there at one point or another. Plus, it was the least gross of all the boys' bathrooms. Prime real estate. He also had a girl he worked with to cover his bases and make sure he wasn't excluding anyone from the opportunity to give him tickets. If Royce had taken over as the top dog, he'd want Choi's spot, too.

When we showed up, it was easy to see that Royce had moved in, because he had merch set up right out in the open where any teacher could see if they'd had a little too much coffee and really needed to go. It was also scattered on the counter and floor, which I was sure was exactly as sanitary it looked.

"Remind me to never eat any of his stuff," I whispered to Conor.

"You already don't," he whispered back.

"Still."

Royce looked like a stick figure—long, straight arms and legs on a long, skinny body. His hair was spiked and he wore a leather jacket that hung loosely on his body, making him seem even more spindly. As he talked to the boy in front of us, he moved with what I'm assuming he thought was a swagger but really just made him look like an out-of-control marionette.

There was another kid with him who I recognized. Jude something. I didn't know him really well—he was a grade below me—but he was a TK. A teacher's kid. So it was a little surprising to see him handing bags to Royce, but not completely. In my experience, most TKs played it pretty straight at school—a consequence of being able to be ratted out to their personal highest authority without even leaving the building. But there was a decent chunk of kids who went in the complete opposite direction and rebelled. He didn't look like he was having a good time rebelling, though. He was a twitchy kid, like a rabbit or a bird or something else that translates to "lunch" in food-chain terms. When he noticed us, he jumped like he was scared he was gonna get caught and looked down at his shoes as he continued slinging sugar.

Conor seemed surprised, too, but for a different reason. "That's new," he said. "Jude didn't used to work for him."

"Business must be booming," I whispered back. It checked out. With his biggest competition knocked out of the game by the mysterious BPS, those customers would have to turn to him if they wanted their sugar fix.

Royce finished up with the customer, exchanging a bag of yellow sugar powder for a string of tickets before flashing a grin at Conor and waving us forward.

"Hey, Conor," he said, spreading a hand to show off the bathroom. "Sweet digs, right? Foot traffic is off the charts! Way better than selling out of my backpack. I mean, I gotta figure out what to do about the girls, but honestly, with the kind of traffic I'm getting, I don't know if I even need them!"

I had a comment to make about the wisdom of excluding literally half the school population from his business plan that I swallowed. That wasn't what we were here for, and if he was so shortsighted, then he deserved to lose out on tickets.

"Congrats, bro," Conor said, nodding at his setup. "Looks like you're all moved in."

"Yeah, yeah. You here to buy? Check it, I just invented a new blend. Lemonade and watermelon. I call it Summer

Pucker Punch. Get it? Cause the lemon makes you pucker? It's crazy awesome."

I could tell that Conor did think it was crazy awesome and not several cavities waiting to happen, but he stayed cool like we talked about and said, "I could try that. Same price?"

"For now. But if it goes good, I'm gonna jack the price way up, so you're lucky you're getting in early."

Again, I didn't think talking to your customers about the price gouging you planned on doing was the best strategy, but it was literally none of my business.

Royce gestured at Jude, who handed him another bag while Conor reached into his pocket and pulled out a wad of tickets, a stick of gum, and half a pencil, which "accidentally" fell out of his stuffed hand, rolling across the bathroom floor to Royce's feet.

"Oh, lemme get . . . that." Royce scooped up the pencil, but as he picked it up, his expression changed and went sly. He straightened and looked at Conor.

"Bro."

"What?"

"Bro," he said, more forcefully.

"What?" Conor said with his trademark Conor teasing.

"Are you . . . you know? Are you?"

"What do you think?" Conor said, nodding at the pencil Royce was still holding.

"I . . . wait." Royce squinted at me. "What about—?"

"Oh, DJ's cool, don't worry," Conor said.

"Not that I don't trust you, but new protocol, I gotta check or I'll get snitched on up the chain to the boss." He flicked his eyes over to Jude. The word *boss* pinged in my head. Did he know who Jude-the-Apparent-Snitch was reporting to? Was finding the mastermind at the heart of this slowly unraveling conspiracy that simple?

Conor nudged me. "Show him."

I dug into my pocket and pulled out my pencil piece. I expected him to give the pencils a once-over and hand them back, but instead, he took mine and gave them both to Jude.

"Do your little scan thing," he said, sounding bored. He turned back to us. "Sorry, this is dumb, but it's a whole thing if I don't do it."

"It's fine," I said, looking over at Jude and swallowing my nervousness as he held the pencils in his cupped hands and pulled a penlight out of his pocket, which he ran over the pencils. What was he looking for? A tiny symbol we'd missed? A certain break pattern? The fake had looked good to me, but if there was more going on than met the eye, then—

"They're good," he said, handing them back to Royce, who handed them back to us.

"See," Royce said, whacking Jude on the shoulder. "Waste of time." But then his eyes lit up. "Anyway, dude! That's so great! Gah, I've been dying not being able to talk to anyone. I mean, like, it's a secret society, I get it, but, like, we can't even know everyone who's in it? That feels like overkill, right?"

And just like that, we had explicit confirmation. There was a secret society, and it was decentralized. No one knew all the members except, I assumed, whoever was at the top.

"Yeah, man," said Conor. "Total overkill."

"When'd you join?" he asked.

"Pretty recently," Conor answered. "Just a few weeks ago."

"Oh! Is that how you've been killing it at the derby? I knew it must be something."

Conor opened his mouth, and I could tell that he

was ready to go off about the fact that he could cheat well enough on his own to dominate Rexcellent without whatever extra help Royce thought he was getting, but I elbowed in and said, "Something like that. And you got Choi's old spot?"

"Yup," he said proudly. "They set him up to get busted for moving sugar, and it was free real estate, baby! Plus, now I have staff," he said, bopping Jude on the head. "Like, he's totally a snitch, but also he has to help me with the merch."

There was our opening. "You say he's snitching. Does that mean you know who he's reporting to? Like you said, it's weird to not know who we're in a group with."

He looked at me, confused. "Uh, yeah I know who the boss is. Don't you?"

"Nah, man," Conor said. "We just joined, remember?"

"But it's so obvious," he said.

"If it's so obvious, then tell us," Conor said, elbowing him playfully, hiding the real burning curiosity behind the words. "Who's the boss?"

"Duh," he said, wiping a line of sugar off the bathroom counter and licking it off his finger. "It's Mariposa."

CHAPTER TWELVE
THE BUTTERFLY EFFECT

I hated that I agreed with Royce. In hindsight, it *was* obvious. Based on what we'd figured out, it seemed like this was an organization that was taking out the best people so the second-best could replace them, and now that we knew about Royce, we knew that the criminal underworld of the school was involved. The number one criminal at school was Lucky, without question, and his second-in-command was Mariposa.

Unlike Lucky, Mariposa didn't go around putting her name on things or throwing her weight around just because, but she ran a lot of what they did behind the scenes, and her lack of visibility, combined with her experience with planning, made her the perfect person to be running a conspiracy of this size so successfully.

I thought about pumping Royce for more info but decided against it. Even though our pencils had passed as proper ID, I didn't want to make the risk of Jude snitching on us higher. Besides, we only had a few minutes before the bell rang, and I wanted to let Audrey and Monty know what we'd found out ASAP.

Usually, there was a good amount of kids hanging out in the field behind school before the bell rang, but it was the middle of winter, so it was freezing. It was one of the safest places to meet without getting spotted. I shot off a text to Audrey and Monty to meet us there after they were done with their recon and was surprised to get an instant *On our way* back from Audrey.

On the way outside, we passed a girl holding a stack of bright blue flyers. I tried to avoid eye contact, but she was a total shark, stepping into our path as soon as we were close.

"Don't forget to nominate Sienna Chase for Snow Princess!"

"I—"

She pressed one of her flyers into my hands and stuck Conor with another one.

"Only one more day of nominations!" she continued cheerily. "You don't wanna miss the deadline!"

"Sure," I said quickly, deciding it was the fastest way to get us out of the one-sided conversation.

"Isn't Sienna that girl whose math test we made disappear?" Conor asked once we were out of earshot. "Shouldn't she be like . . . studying?"

I shrugged. "Hey, she has someone else delivering her flyers. Maybe she *is* studying." I didn't want him to remember that he'd made it his mission to get me to take Audrey to the dance, so I chucked the flyer in the nearest trash can and picked up speed. "We should hurry. The rest of the team is waiting for us."

When we got outside, we saw them both standing near an iced-over tree. Monty's army jacket hung on Audrey's frame, over her coat, while Monty stood bare armed, keeping watch.

"Dude, aren't you cold?" Conor asked.

Monty pointed at himself at the same time Audrey did and they said "Canadian" in unison. Audrey smiled slightly, like she'd had the same conversation with Monty just before we'd shown up.

"Oh, right. Forgot you're a polar bear."

"You guys got here fast," I said. "Did you finish up at a cappella already?"

Audrey made a face. "It didn't go how I'd hoped. We got flyers, but a cappella meets the same time as drama. I'd have to miss meetings if I joined. I can if you really need me to, but—"

"Don't bother," I said. "We got what we needed from Royce. Full verbal confirmation."

"He just told you?"

"Spilled his guts," I said. "Didn't even need your skills. We did need the pencils, though, so good job, Monty. Worked like a charm."

He beamed.

"That's not even the wildest part," Conor said. "Get this. According to him, the leader of the operation is Mariposa."

"Oh!" Monty said, grabbing Audrey's shoulder excitedly. "Oh! Tell DJ what you told me!"

Her eyes lit up. "Oh, right! Guys, remember that job we did right after the Starcade Job? That kid who was gonna get busted for stealing from Lucky?"

I nodded. Of course I remembered. It was our first job as an official team. "Kiley Davenport. We found the merch, cleared her, and Arlo Stevenson got rocket boosted instead."

"Right. But Kiley? Captain of the dance team. She wasn't on our list because she wasn't replaced, but if she'd been rocket boosted—"

"She probably would have quit," Conor cut in. "Hard to be all smiley and jazz handsy and covered in glitter when no one will talk to you."

"I was thinking that it might be something to add to your list. A botched attempt at taking her out. And if you're saying Mariposa is involved . . ."

"Then it would be super easy for her to arrange to have the stuff stolen herself and accuse Kiley," I said. "You're right. That fits the pattern. And she'd have access to your cheats, Conor. Maybe she's behind that, too."

"We gotta move quick, right?" Conor asked. "On Mariposa, I mean. While she doesn't have Lucky to back her up." He suddenly stopped, eyes bugging out.

"What?" I asked.

"Are we sure she didn't . . . you know?"

"I know what?"

"Arrange a little *accident* for Lucky on the slopes."

"Oh, come on," Audrey said. "That was in a whole other state. She wasn't even there. There's no way."

She hesitated before looking over to me. "Right?"

"Right," I confirmed, even though I couldn't help but feel like if there was anyone at our school who could pull it off—including the teachers—it was probably her. I shook my head of the thought. Something that drastic didn't seem to fit the group's MO. They were breaking pottery, not people.

"Let's assume the broken leg is just a normal broken leg for now. Lucky's only gonna be on bed rest for so long, so we don't have a ton of time. We need to move fast. But we need a way to get her dead to rights. It's not gonna be like Royce. We can't just ask her, 'Hey, are you running a criminal operation on the side of your other criminal operation?'"

"Can't we?" Monty asked. "I mean, not all of us," he added quickly when I gave him my best *Dude, what?* face. "Just Audrey. Can't she go talk to Mariposa? But in a Face-y kind of way."

"That's not a bad idea," said Conor. "Audrey can go to Mariposa, pretend to want to join. I can hook her up for sound. We record the whole thing and boom. We got her."

I had been picturing a more drawn-out operation

involving tailing and careful observation, but Conor was right. If anyone could get away with just asking Mariposa point-blank, it was Audrey. And it would be a lot faster—which was good if we wanted to try to stop whatever schemes they had cooking at the moment before the list of bumped-off number ones got even higher. Or more selfishly—before one of us wound up on the menu.

"That could work," I said under my breath, puffs of condensation leaving my mouth like chimney smoke as I muttered to myself, trying to work out logistics. "With Lucky out, she has so much extra stuff on her plate. I bet she's off her game. Which is still better than most people's games, but we'll take what we can get. And I know none of us are big fans of Lucky, but the enemy of my enemy . . . If he finds out that his second-in-command is heading a secret organization that takes out all the number one people in the school, he might have some kind of problem about that."

"And then the problem takes care of itself," said Conor. "That's smart."

"But, Audrey," I said, turning to her. "You'd be the one actually doing it. What do you think?"

She'd already looked plenty warm with her double-coat situation, but somehow, she looked even warmer now. Her smile lit up her eyes, and it made me feel toasty just looking at her. "I think it's a great idea!"

"Yeah?"

"Yeah! And it will finally burn me. Lucky will know I work with you guys. Then we can hang out at school!"

The warmth I'd felt seemed to disappear, and I could feel the winter air around me sharper than ever. "I—I thought you didn't mind not hanging out at school."

She shrugged. "I mean, it's for the good of the team so it's fine, but I'd rather hang out with you guys."

Conor shot me a look that I ignored.

"Um . . . OK, great. That's . . . right. Well, we have to figure out a time to talk to her."

"I can figure out a way to get into the cafeteria during your lunch period," Audrey offered. "I know she does business then."

"It would be better if you could talk to her off campus," I said. "This is her home turf. You'd have an easier time somewhere she'd be more off-balance. Less in her element."

"What about the Starcade?" Conor asked.

I wrinkled my nose. "Mariposa doesn't go to the Starcade." I'd never seen her there, and word was, even though she was surrounded by the spoils of the place all the time, she didn't actually participate in the fun and games. Strictly management.

"No, but Lucky does, right?" said Conor. "Once a week to make sure no one's cracked your Rowdy Roundup exploit. And if Lucky's out—"

"Then it'll go to her," I finished. "Unless she delegates, but I'm pretty sure she won't. They don't want to send someone to do that every week and maybe start asking questions. We don't know if she's already been to the Starcade for the week yet, though. And she might not go until the weekend. Unless we can figure out a way to get her there faster."

"Mariposa's aunt drives her home," Audrey said. "You know, the one who works in the front office? Mrs. Delgado. And she leaves, like, right when the bell rings. I would, too, if I worked here, honestly."

"So the Starcade is out," I said, gearing up to move to a new tactic, but Audrey stopped me.

"I didn't say that. Mariposa is a tricky target, but I think I can still get her to the Starcade. Today, if you want. I just need an excuse to go to the front office and for Conor to sneak into the teachers' lounge to grab something from the trash."

He made a face. "Why am I always the trash guy?"

"Because you're so good at it!" Audrey said, patting him once on the cheek. She opened her mouth again, but the bell rang, drowning out the first words of her sentence.

"Ugh, gotta make myself scarce," Audrey said. Then she grinned. "But not for long! I'll text you guys the plan. See you after school!"

At lunch, Conor and I sat together, watching Mariposa from across the room. People had been coming in to talk to her all period, including people who didn't even have lunch that period. With Lucky gone, she was handling all of his business in addition to hers. I didn't recognize the girl she was talking to. She was short, with thick, round glasses and bangs that she kept brushing out of her face. Was she a prospective BPS member? Were they having a recruitment meeting right now? She wasn't someone I would peg at a glance as a member of a criminal operation, but I wouldn't suspect Kennedy of anything other than turning in her homework early, either. It could be anyone. Or it could be a totally random conversation. There was no way to tell without getting way closer to Mariposa than I was comfortable with. This Starcade operation was crucial.

Conor checked the time and grabbed his backpack. "Lunch is almost over. I gotta deliver the goods to Audrey. This is a good plan."

"Yeah," I said. "It should work." I looked down and back up, expecting him to be gone when I did, but he was still looking at me. "What?"

"Audrey's smart."

"I know."

"And good at this."

"I know."

"Aaaaand?"

"And what, Conor?"

He rolled his eyes and chuckled, pulling an orange coffee cup out of his backpack. "Forget it, man. I'll see you later."

* * *

After school, I checked my texts and then made for the Starcade as quickly as possible. When I reached the parking lot, I smiled. Mrs. Delgado's car was parked right in front of Bean There, Done That, the trendy little coffee shop next to the Starcade. The thing that Audrey had asked Conor to swipe from the trash was a coffee cup from the teachers' lounge. It was a safe bet that one would be there. The bright orange cups were really easy to spot in the hands of teachers blearily walking into the building or coming back from their lunch breaks. The kids at the Fitz might run on Starcade tickets, but the adults ran on Bean There coffee. And, luckily, those two businesses were next to each other.

I was the last one to show up. Conor and Audrey were in the Starcade alley waiting for me, and I knew Monty was in the coffee shop, already on comms and holding up the line. There were a lot of options on the menu, and he was under instructions to ask about all of them until we told him to stop.

When Audrey saw me walk up, she did a huge mock bow. "Thank you, thank you. Hold your applause."

"We're gonna have to get her a lightsaber," Conor said. "Jedi Master Audrey with her mind trick."

"Aww, it wasn't that hard. I know Mrs. Delgado likes peppermint mocha lattes. You can smell them as soon as you walk in the office. Holding the cup while talking to her for a few minutes about the peppermint chocolate stocking stuffers I got for Christmas was a no-brainer. And they're limited edition! Gotta get 'em fast."

"Is Mariposa in there?"

"Yup," Audrey said. "We'll all be on a call, so you'll be able to talk to me and hear at least my side of the conversation. And Conor has my phone set up with the recording software and the little mic upgrade, so if she says anything we can use, I'll get it. I was just waiting for you all before I went in."

"You all set on the plan?" I asked, slipping in the earbuds that Conor handed to me.

"Yeah, I'm gonna use the musical," she said. "I can act upset that I didn't get the role I wanted. That gives me a reason to want in. And I can say I found out about it from Duncan. Choir and band kids hang out enough that it wouldn't be suspicious."

I nodded. "Perfect. Conor, I want you in there with her, as backup." I almost wanted to send in Monty for maximum protection, but he was kind of hard to miss. I didn't want Mariposa's suspicions even slightly raised.

"Don't worry about anything you say to DJ on comms before you get to Mariposa," Conor said. "I'll just cut it out before we send it to Lucky."

"And let us know if you need us to bail you out," I said.

"Don't worry," she said. "I got this. Just stay out of the way so she doesn't see you when she walks out."

With that, we rounded back to the front of the Starcade. Conor slipped in first and made his way to the boys' bathroom—the one place we could be 99.9 percent sure Mariposa wouldn't be. A few seconds later, Audrey walked in.

"Ah, OK, I'm not seeing her," I heard Audrey say, voice low.

"She's probably near the Rowdy Roundup machine," I said. "Check there."

"Mmm, I'm still not— Oh, she's in a booth. OK, awesome, I'm just gonna slide right in."

"Mariposa, right?" I heard her say; I could picture her flashing her signature disarming grin. "I always see you at school with the super-cute butterfly tattoos. Do you get them here?"

Even though Audrey was hooked up for sound, I couldn't hear Mariposa's response over the loudness of the arcade. Mariposa was scary, but she was also pretty soft-spoken, which honestly made her more scary. Annoying, but I trusted Audrey could handle herself, and I was pretty good at figuring out what was going on from hearing just one side of the conversation.

There was a pause and then Audrey said, "Well, of course not, but there's never been a good time before. When else would I catch you alone?"

Another pause, then Audrey laughed.

"Aw, thanks! Yeah, that was really fun. I worked hard for that solo. Luckily, you can do that in choir. Less political, you know? I mean, people still butt heads but not like in drama. I mean, it's literally in the name. Total drama city. No matter how good you are." She launched into a story I'd heard many times before about the first drama club production at the Fitz years ago. Apparently, between act one and act two of *Annie Jr.*, Annie's understudy had yanked the red wig off Annie's head in a fit of jealousy and tried to flush it down the toilet. It wasn't actually a huge secret, but Audrey was telling it like it was. That was the trick. Let people think you were letting them in on your secrets and they were more likely to let you in on theirs.

As she finished the anecdote she said, "I've heard it's like that in other clubs, too. Like band. In fact, I was talking to Duncan the other day. You know. Second-chair tuba. Well, first chair now. Funny, right? Kinda makes you wonder how that happened, huh?"

I hadn't been able to hear anything else Mariposa had said all conversation, but her next sentence was so clear that I heard it with no problem.

"They got to *you*?"

"I—uh, huh?" I'd never heard Audrey break during a job before, but I could tell, she wasn't acting. She was reacting. Which would have been troubling in and of itself, but then something worse happened. She went silent. Not only was she not talking, all the ambient noise from her side of the call went dead.

"Did we lose her?" said Conor. "Should I jump in? I'm gonna jump in."

"Wait," I said sharply. "We don't know what's happening in there. We don't want to rush in and blow it. Maybe she has it under control. We should give her a minute."

"But what if she's in trouble?" Conor said.

I hesitated but then remembered the hallway lollipop incident. "Audrey can handle being in trouble for a minute, but once we blow it, it's blown. Just wait a minute."

I counted down the seconds. Sixty. Forty-five. Thirty.

"Forget that. I'm going in."

"Conor? *Conor!*" But it was too late. I heard the bathroom door slam, and the sounds of the game floor started up again. I made a split-second decision and ran into the Starcade. Maybe I could stop him if I just—

And then I heard a voice over comms. "DJ. I know you can hear me."

I froze in my tracks. It was Mariposa.

"Tomorrow morning. Front office at the top of breakfast. All four of you. And if you're late, you're all getting rocket boosted."

And then the line went dead.

CHAPTER THIRTEEN
THE BREAKFAST CLUB

I dove behind an arcade cabinet before Mariposa could see me as she walked out. Not that it would have mattered much—she clearly already knew I was around. But I didn't want her to see I'd completely lost my poker face.

What was that? What had just happened?

"Audrey, are you—" Conor started, but she jumped in quickly.

"I'm fine, I'm fine. But I—" She stopped. "Everyone, head to my house. We can talk there."

"Are you—"

"Just go to my house," she said again, this time cutting off Monty. "I'll meet you there."

"You heard her," I said. "Monty, leave your money in the tip jar and bail." We figured we should compensate the underpaid barista for wasting their time.

"Get off comms. We'll meet back at Audrey's."

It took everything in me to not just follow directly behind Audrey as she left the Starcade, but I let her and Conor leave first before heading in the same direction. About ten minutes later, we were all at Audrey's place, sitting around her coffee table.

Audrey had taken out cookie dough, and the oven was open like she'd thought about putting it in, but she was just popping the raw squares into her mouth.

"I'm so sorry, you guys," she said around a mouth of sugary dough and chocolate chips. "I broke. That was such a rookie mistake."

"Hey, hey," I said. "Don't beat yourself up."

"Yeah," said Conor, ripping off a chunk of dough and cramming it into his mouth. "I screw up all the time."

"All the time," I echoed.

"Hey!"

"What exactly happened, though?" I asked. "To make you break, I mean. We couldn't really hear her side of the conversation. Did she threaten you or something?"

"She threatened you?" Monty said, his voice squeaking more than usual.

"No, no," Audrey said quickly, patting him on the arm. "Nothing like that. She just . . . The reason I was caught so off guard is because *she* was caught so off guard. I thought we were playing coy, but I saw the look on her face. She wasn't playing games—she was actually surprised."

"I would act surprised, too, if someone was hinting that they knew I was doing something I shouldn't be doing," Conor pointed out.

Audrey shook her head adamantly. "No. You guys didn't see her. She's not a part of it . . . but she does know what it is. At least partially. She said, 'They got to *you*?'"

"Yeah, we heard that part," I said. "Or at least I did."

"She said 'they.' Meaning other than her. And whatever it is, it's something she thinks I wouldn't be tangled up in."

"Well, yeah," Conor said. "She didn't know you ran with us until you told her."

Audrey paused for a second, pressed her lips together, and squinted out into the middle distance.

"What?" I asked. I knew that look. That's how she looked when she was about to . . . not lie but give information in what she thought was the least distressing way possible.

"Yeah, about that. I *didn't* tell her."

"What? But she knew we were there. All four of us. If you didn't tell her, then how did she know?"

"Duke did film us a bunch at the Starcade party," said Monty. "Maybe she figured it out from that."

Mariposa did a lot of the nitty-gritty work for the operation while Lucky was doing the front-facing work. I could see him letting her review the footage and filling him in on the important details. "But if she figured it out from Duke's footage, wouldn't she have told Lucky?"

"Not if she wanted to keep it a secret," said Audrey. "Something in her back pocket in case she could use it later."

"Knowledge is power," I said. "Could be it." I wasn't sure if I should be grateful Mariposa hadn't exposed Audrey as soon as she'd found out, or worried that she still could at any moment. Although maybe I should have been more worried about the fact that she'd threatened to rocket boost all of us if we didn't meet with her in the morning.

"OK," I said. "I don't think we really have a choice. We have to go to that meeting in the morning. And, even if we didn't, I still think it would be a good idea. She wants to talk to us, and she probably has info that we don't. Maybe we can make a trade, or if not that, maybe she'll let something slip."

"Do you want me to do most of the talking, or do you want to do it?" Audrey asked.

"I'll talk," I said. "She'll probably wanna talk to me anyway. We've talked before. I want you set to human lie detector."

"Can do," she said.

"And, Monty, this is prime soft-muscle time. We don't actually have a lot of leverage here, but it never hurts to go into a meeting with some muscle in your corner."

"What about me?" said Conor. "What should I do?"

"Keep your mouth shut so you don't stick your foot in it," I said.

He crossed his arms. "Well, if you're so good at talking, what are you gonna tell her?"

"That's a good point," I said. "We should get our story straight." I paused as I thought. "OK, we'll tell her as little as possible. That we heard about an organization called the BPS and we thought she might have something to do with it. Not a lie, but not everything we know. If you think she's on the level, flash me a signal and I'll tell her more."

"Ooh, are we doing secret-code stuff now?" Conor said, perking up. "Like a secret code word? Should I get my spy kit? Night-vision goggles, invisible-ink pens—"

"Conor, how would either of those things help us?"

"Spy tools are cool," he mumbled, shoving another glob of cookie dough into his mouth.

I turned back to Audrey.

"I think you can just nod," I said. "No reason to make things more complicated."

She sighed dramatically. "The secret organizations get to have all the fun."

We talked a little bit longer and planned to meet in the office before it started so we could walk in together. United front and all that. I arranged to get a ride with Conor instead of taking the bus. We could *not* be late for this. We were on shaky footing as is.

As we walked into the front office the next day, I almost felt like I should be wearing armor or that black stuff football players put under their eyes before a game. This was Mariposa. One wrong move and she could have us rocket boosted. We didn't have room for error.

"United front," I said quietly, waiting for nods from everyone before I swung open the door to the front office.

Mariposa hadn't given us directions for what to do when we arrived at the front office, but I assumed we were supposed to talk to her aunt. That ended up being unnecessary, because Mrs. Delgado flagged us down as soon as we walked in.

"There you are," she said brightly. "Posa said some of her friends would be stopping by for a playdate."

I had to actively stop myself from snorting. Did Al Capone's aunt set him up on playdates, too?

"Posa?" Conor mouthed, and I nudged him in the ribs as Audrey said, "Yeah! She said to meet her here. Do you know where she is?"

"Second door on the right," Mrs. Delgado said, pointing down the hall. "I helped her set up. She's really excited to— Oh, but look at me spoiling the surprise." She mimed locking her lips and throwing away the key.

"Second door to the right," Audrey repeated. "Thanks, Mrs. Delgado!"

"Have fun!" she called back as we made our way to the lion's den.

The placard outside the door said it was a conference room. Maybe a lesser-used one she knew she could commandeer? Or had she gotten her aunt to properly book the room? I shook my head. *Focus, DJ.* That was the least of our worries. What really mattered was—

Before I could get my train of thought back on track or grab the handle of the door, it swung open on its own, revealing Mariposa, arms folded, butterfly tattoo on her upper arm, hot pink blouse contrasted by her cool gaze.

"You're here," she said. "Good. Arranging four rocket boostings this week would have been annoying." What a way to describe the complete social annihilation of four people: *annoying*.

She moved out of the way and gestured toward the table at the center of the room, and suddenly I understood what her aunt meant by setup. The cafeteria food was pretty mediocre at the Fitz, but one thing the cafeteria did well was French toast sticks. Golden brown, just the right amount of sugar and cinnamon—they even tasted pretty good cold.

At the table were four place settings. At each was a double portion of French toast sticks and at the center was a pyramid of maple syrup cups. The cafeteria had a strict limit of one per person, which wasn't nearly enough for one serving of French toast sticks, even with careful rationing. There were more syrup cups in that pile than a kid would see in a month. I suddenly had a better idea of what that business transaction I'd seen between her and the mousy kid in the cafeteria had been about.

I glanced over at Conor, and I swear, I saw his eyes dilate. When I gave him a tiny headshake, he pouted. I didn't think the food was poisoned or anything. But this was clearly a show of power, and an attempt to make us drop our guard. I wasn't falling for it.

Mariposa stared us down until we took our seats, and then she stood—not sat, stood—at the head of the table.

"Well?" she said. "What do you have to say for yourselves? Talk."

"OK, here's the deal—" I started, but I was cut off as she raised a hand and shook her head slightly.

"Not you," said Mariposa. "And I don't want to hear it from either of them," she said, flicking a finger between

Audrey and Conor. "You're tricky, she lies professionally, and he annoys me."

"I—"

Mariposa and I shushed Conor at the same time. He frowned but shut up, defiantly snatching a French toast stick from his plate and sticking it into his mouth, syrupless.

"I want to know exactly what it is you four thought you were doing baiting me in the middle of that Starcade, and I want Monty to tell me."

My poker face stayed solid, but I could feel my insides start dissolving. Monty had been around for the planning conversation, but he wasn't on the list of talkers. He was never on the list of talkers.

"Me?" he squeaked.

And for good reason.

I gestured toward him casually, with fake confidence. "Sure. Tell her, Monty."

Don't spill your guts, I chanted in my head. *Stick to the story, stick to the story, stick to the—*

"Uh, DJ got a note about something called the BPS and there was a broken pencil taped to it but it was a number one pencil, which is weird, right? Have you ever seen a number one pencil? I hadn't. DJ thought it had something to do with this kid from his old school because he showed up here out of nowhere, but now we're thinking that was probably a coincidence. Anyway, we think the BPS is doing some bad stuff and getting rid of all the number one people to replace them with the number two people and a lot of people are involved, like Kennedy and Duncan and Royce and a bunch of others—DJ has a list—and we thought you were in charge, so we sent Audrey to check, but she said you weren't, and then you made us come here." He turned back to me. "Did I miss anything?"

"Nope," I said, trying to not grind my teeth. I grabbed a syrup cup from the stack and ripped it open. No point in depriving myself now. "You told her just about everything."

Mariposa smirked. "Well, that was thorough."

Boy, was it ever.

"And it makes sense that you thought that I was involved. But I'm not."

"But Royce said you were," Conor chimed in.

"Royce is an idiot," she shot back.

Harsh, but I wouldn't exactly argue with her.

"Why would you listen to anything he said?" Mariposa asked.

"We confirmed he's in the group," I said, picking up the narration. I figured that if she didn't shut down Conor, she wouldn't shut me down, and Monty had pretty much given up all our secrets. "It was the best lead we had." I decided to push a little further. "And it wasn't a total dead end, seeing as you're saying you're not in it but you clearly know what it is."

She seemed to consider me for a moment, and then she reached under the table and pulled out a sheet of printer paper. Taped to it was a number one pencil, identical to the one we'd used to make our fake and matching the half I'd gotten in my locker.

"Someone slipped this in my locker on Monday," she said, handing it to me.

The rest of the crew crowded around me to read it over my shoulder:

The undeserving get the glory while those in the shadows toil in silence. The just should be rewarded while just desserts are served. Seize the opportunity. Take control.

Go from number 2 to number 1. Join the Broken Pencil Society.

"'Broken Pencil Society,'" Audrey read out loud. "BPS. That's it!"

Conor laughed.

"What?" she asked.

"Number two."

Audrey rolled her eyes. "Conor, please."

"This is a recruitment letter," I said.

Mariposa nodded. "Of course they'd send it to me when Lucky was out on bed rest. In case I was too chicken to betray him while he was around." She sneered. "It's insulting. If I wanted to betray Lucky, I'd do it to his face."

I flicked a glance over at Audrey, who stopped dunking a French toast stick and nodded a quick confirmation that she was being dead serious. I said a mental thanks that Mariposa wasn't currently mad at *us*.

"What's with the pencil?" Conor asked. "Aren't they supposed to be broken?"

"Only if I join," she said. "I'm supposed to break it and put it in locker forty-two if I join, and then they fill me in on the details. Whoever 'they' are. This is the first I've heard of it, but once I started thinking about it, I realized the landscape has changed over the past few months. You already know about Choi since you talked to Royce. And there have been shake-ups in other arenas, too. Hall pass forgery. Test postponements. Essay ghostwriting. Things do just change, but I don't like this. I don't like the idea of someone manipulating the balance of things."

Someone who isn't you or Lucky, you mean, I thought but didn't say.

"So, you're against them?" Monty asked.

"Of course," said Mariposa.

Monty brightened. "Oh! Then we can work together!"

Conor scoffed. "There is no way that—"

"No, he's right," Mariposa said. "Our interests are aligned, and I'd like to get this cleaned up before Lucky gets back, if possible. He doesn't always . . . appreciate the subtle solution to a problem."

That tracked with my last experience with him. But that still gave me some pause. "So you're not going to tell him?"

"I tell Lucky everything he needs to know," she said, glancing over at Audrey pointedly before looking back at me. "I'd rather him go in guns blazing for cleanup *after* we get to the bottom of this."

That meant we were on the same page. I didn't approve of a lot of how Lucky handled things, but this was one of those situations that I felt basically equaled out to zero, karma-wise.

"Do you know when Lucky will be back?" I asked.

"He's pushing it as long as he can, so we have some time," Mariposa replied. "But not unlimited time, so we'll need to be efficient."

"We can share information," I said. "Well, you just heard most of ours, and we have that list of possible members Monty mentioned. Oh, and relevant to you. We think at least one of them tried to force a rocket boosting back in December."

She frowned. "Davenport. Stolen box of merch. I remember that. I thought it felt fishy." I could see her make a mental note, and I felt the tiniest bit of sympathy for whoever was behind that one.

"Conor's also pretty sure they're messing with TEC derby races," I added. "Not that you have *anything* to do with those. But if you wanna let Miguel know then—"

"I'll make sure it's handled."

Conor flashed me a grateful look. He'd been running out of excuses to dodge a rematch with Ambrose. He opened his mouth like he was gonna say something but then realized his mouth was full and that he was in spraying distance of Mariposa and thought better of it, chewing and swallowing first.

"Have you thought about a stakeout?" Conor asked. "You drop the pencil, someone has to pick it up."

"I thought about it," she said, "but I have to leave school right after it's over 'cause I go home with my aunt"—she squinted at me—"which you already know. And I didn't trust anyone else to get involved."

"We can help!" Monty said eagerly, like this was a fun group project and not a dubious alliance with the second-most notorious criminal on campus.

"He's right," Audrey said. "I bet I could stay late today if I text my parents. What about you guys?"

"I'm game," Monty said.

"Me too," I added. "Conor?"

He shook his head. "Baby sister has a dance recital, and we all have to go. I have to leave right after the bell rings."

"Well, that's three of us," I said. "You said locker forty-two, right? That's in the main hallway. I think the origami club and the board game club meet there."

All this research had left us with a pretty good working knowledge of what all the clubs on campus were doing.

"Those are both drop in, drop out. You don't need to be an official member to join. We can crash the meetings today and keep watch."

Mariposa nodded. "We'll have a call after school. You don't have to call me; I'll call you."

For a second, I wondered how she was going to do that without us giving her our numbers, but then I remembered who we were talking to.

Right. Her aunt works in the front office. She probably has access to everyone's numbers.

"Tell me what you find out," she continued. "I'll do the same. And if you tell anyone we're working together, you're all gone by the next school day."

I knew from experience when a threat meant "goodbye." We filed out of the room—Conor stuffing his mouth and taking a handful of syrup cups for the road, Monty waving like he'd taken the playdate thing seriously.

I gathered my thoughts. The meeting hadn't been bad. Weird, but not bad. My biggest fear had been that she'd rocket boost us, and instead she'd . . . fed us and offered to work with us. Something in the back of my mind twinged with . . . guilt? Not quite that but something close to it. Doing what we did meant I was walking the line between good kid and bad guy every day. Did working with Mariposa tip the scales? I didn't think so. But I wasn't exactly a Boy Scout. I tried to shake off the thought. That was a David question. I had a job to do, and the faster it got done, the faster we'd be done with this sketchy alliance.

"OK," I said. "Audrey and Monty, you're on origami after school. And I'll play some games. Let's do this."

CHAPTER FOURTEEN
HAIL TO THE CHIEF

Unlike the chess club, the board game club was pretty chill. There weren't official competitions or rankings. You just showed up and played some games. Mr. Anderson—a math teacher—supervised, which meant he just drank coffee and listened to podcasts while the students did whatever they wanted. When I arrived, there was already a game of UNO starting up, a girl unboxing a Sorry! board, and a cluster of kids setting up a map for Dungeons & Dragons.

None of the positions seemed optimal for watching the hall, so I grabbed a pack of cards and set up by myself where I had a better view.

"Hey," said the girl with the Sorry! board, "do you wanna play? I only have two friends coming."

"No thanks," I said. "I'm playing solitaire."

"Alone?"

"It's a one-player game."

"Huh," she said before shrugging. "All right. Have fun."

I actually didn't know how to play solitaire, but based on her reaction, I doubted anyone else here did, either, so I fanned out the cards in front of me and made myself look busy while I kept an eye on the hall through the door's window slit. Monty and Audrey were doing the same across the hall—minus the deck of cards, I assumed.

It wasn't the most exciting thing in the world, but everything can't be ticket heists and Moonwalking Bears. Sometimes crime is boring.

Boring enough to give you time to think.

I'd tried to put it out of my mind until later because we had a truce with Mariposa, so technically it didn't matter, but I couldn't shake the thought.

All these weeks of being so careful, and it turned out Audrey was already on Mariposa's radar. What was the point? Was it even worth trying to keep it secret? Audrey hadn't said anything since we'd found out, but she'd practically cheered the idea of being burned, and now it turned out she already was? I could feel an "I told you so" in my future, except I knew Audrey would never say it, even if I deserved it.

I knew she understood about the team and the mission and all, and that I was only trying to keep everyone safe, but—

Someone was approaching. Were they going for the locker? No, they were stopping at our room. The door swung open and in walked Tessa, clipboard under her arm. She walked over to Mr. Anderson, and they talked for a little bit. Then she began bopping from group to group, talking to them and then scribbling on her clipboard. Student gov stuff. Not my problem.

I ignored her and kept staring into the hallway until a few minutes later when I heard the clack of plastic being placed on the desk next to mine.

When I turned, I saw that Tessa had set down a Connect 4 game and was racking it up.

"Hey there!" she said, Disney Channel smile at full brightness. "You wanna play a quick game?"

"Nah, I'm good," I said, pointing to my cards.

"Oh, come on," she said, sitting down at the desk. "I can't just let you play alone. I'm class president. I need to make sure everyone's having a good time." She held up her clipboard. "That's why I'm checking out all the clubs and taking surveys."

I wanted to tell her that I would be having a much better time if she'd just get out of my way and stop blocking my view, but I didn't wanna be mean to her, and I figured playing a game of Connect 4 was the fastest way to exit the conversation.

"OK, we can play one round. And then back to solitaire."

"Great! Red or yellow?" She held up two pieces and I picked the red one. "You can go first."

I dropped the piece into the center of the board. "So, you're just checking out all the different clubs?"

"Mm-hm!" she said, making her move. "Lunch clubs and after-school ones, too."

I thought about the laundry list of clubs I'd recently learned the Fitz had.

"That sounds like a lot of work," I said.

"It is," she said, "but it's important!"

"Is this part of the job, or did you decide to do it on your own?"

"It was my idea," she confirmed. "I tried to suggest it when I was VP last year, but my sister didn't go for it. I think she thought it was too much work, but being president comes with responsibility. Like, I'm coming in before school on Tuesday to work on decorations for the dance 'cause we have Monday off for MLK Day. I don't have to, but Caro is having some of the Space Cadets come in, and if they are, I should, too."

I was pretty sure she was putting more effort into this student government thing than some people in the actual government, but I wasn't about to rag on her for being *too* competent.

"And besides," she said, "I'm not doing these surveys alone. Paige is helping. We split it up, half and half. I think she's in the origami club right now. Hey, speaking of, do you mind if I ask you some questions while we play?"

I shrugged. "Go for it."

She shotgunned questions at me between moves.

"How are you enjoying the board game club?"

"Do you feel like your voice is being heard?"

"Do you have any suggestions on how to improve the club?"

By the time she was done, the board was full, and neither of us had managed to follow the one instruction in the name of the game.

"A draw," I said, impressed. "You're good at this."

She smiled. "Yeah, I have a lot of practice. It's my sister's favorite, and she always got to pick the game. You know how it is with older siblings."

"I'm an only child."

"Heh, well. Thanks for doing the survey!" She got up and moved to the next kid.

I watched the hall for the rest of the club, but no one came to pick up the pencil, and we could only hang around for so long. Conor was out, so we decided to just go home instead of having a group meeting. We had the long weekend for a proper meeting if we needed it.

About an hour after I got home, I got a link for a video call from a number I didn't recognize.

Mariposa.

There wasn't a time attached, which I assumed was her subtle way of saying, "If you're not on in the next five seconds, you're toast."

I logged on.

I was the first one. Mariposa was in her house—or maybe her aunt's house—sitting in a big easy chair that should have made her look tiny but honestly just made her look like she was sitting on a throne.

"DJ," she said.

"Mariposa," I said back, texting the gang just off camera to tell them to hurry up and log on.

One by one, everyone else filtered in, Conor showing up last, in a bathroom stall and wearing a collared shirt that I know his mom must have forced him into.

"Good," Mariposa said. "Let's make this quick. Did you learn anything?"

"Nothing," I said. "No one came to pick up the pencil. Maybe it's biweekly, or they pick it up on a different day? Or it could be at a different time. It was a long shot, but now it's a dead end."

"Well, that was a total waste of time," Mariposa said, as if it had been her time that was wasted.

"Not totally!" Monty said, pulling a wad of paper out of his pocket. No, it wasn't just one wad, it was a stack of origami pieces.

Mariposa looked at him like he was out of his mind, then said, "Is he serious?"

I shrugged. That was Monty. Hopefully we never needed to try to use him to intimidate her, because that cat was out of the bag.

"I was gonna show you guys on Tuesday, but I don't want this meeting to be pointless." He started passing his creations in front of the camera. "See, Conor, I made you a frog. It jumps."

"That's sick. Thanks, man."

"And a bird for DJ. The wings flap."

"Dope. Thanks, Monty."

"And I already gave Audrey her flower."

"Which is still in my hair," Audrey said, pointing it out with a grin. "You're the best, Monty."

Mariposa rolled her eyes. "If we're done with Secret Santa, we can—"

"Wait," said Monty. "I made you one, too. See?" He held up a purple butterfly.

She looked at it like it might explode. "You made that for me?"

"Yeah!" he said, pushing it toward the camera. "Look, I put glitter on it, too!"

"Why?"

"Because you like glitter."

"No, why did you make one for me?"

"I made them for everyone!"

She made a face that clearly said, *Since when am I a part of everyone?* but just coughed and said, "Uh, sure. Anyway, nothing else happened?"

"No," I said again. "Just board games. And an interview with Tessa about my feelings about this club I'm not actually in."

"Oh, Paige did the same thing to us," Audrey pointed out. "It's apparently a new initiative."

Conor snorted. "Man, Tessa's always doing the most, huh? Back at the Grove, our student council did basically nothing except have pizza parties we weren't invited to. Meanwhile, Tessa is almost busier than Lucky."

He was right. Student government tended to be mostly symbolic while the real power lay elsewhere, but Tessa bucked that trend. At the Fitz, the aboveground was a mirror of the underground. Lucky and Mariposa. Tessa and . . .

"Paige," I said softly, feeling a jolt go down my spine. How had we missed something so obvious? We'd suspected

Mariposa because she was second to Lucky, the most powerful criminal at school. But if it wasn't her . . .

"What about Paige?" Mariposa said, suddenly leaning forward in her seat. She could tell I was onto something.

"We thought it was you because you're Lucky's go-to person and he's the number one guy. Vice president is literally your job, but legit. If it's not you—"

"Oh!" Monty said, eyes widening. "That's so smart!"

"And it makes sense," Conor added. "I'd totally be jealous if I was Tractor Tran and I had to follow behind Tessa all the time."

"Conor!" Audrey said sharply.

"What?"

"Her name is Paige!"

"She doesn't care! She goes by that. Also, if DJ's right, and he usually is, she got like a ton of people kicked out of their positions, so I don't think what we call her is the biggest thing here."

"I don't know much about Paige," said Mariposa. "But most people don't know much about me. She has the power and access of student gov but not a lot of visibility. She's perfect for this."

"Uh, guys," said Monty. "If Paige is doing what we thought Mariposa was doing and we thought Mariposa was going to take down Lucky, does that mean Paige is going after Tessa?"

"That's what I'm worried about," I said. "We should talk to Tessa, but we need a good excuse. Like, if we could interview her the way she did to me."

"What about for the school paper?" Mariposa asked.

"We don't have a school paper," I said.

"We can by Tuesday," Mariposa shot back. "Just tell me who you want in the club on the record and I can make it official."

"It's gotta be Audrey, right?" said Conor. "This is her whole thing."

"Oh!" Audrey said, clapping her hands together. "This will be fun! I get to go all Mary Sunshine and do the softball-question thing."

"Can you add me, too?" I asked. "I want to go with her."

Audrey perked up. "Really? But you always say . . ."

"If we're both in the same club, it's a good enough reason for us to be hanging together. Like when we did the musical. And I don't want to send you in alone for this."

She looked even more excited. "This is great! You can be my photographer or something!"

I was happy to see her pumped, but I couldn't go gooey in the middle of a planning sesh. "We'll try to figure out what she knows and if she's in any danger. It's really easy for people to walk around with a sword hanging over their head without realizing it if they never look up."

"It would be less from above and more from behind," said Mariposa. "I don't know a lot about Paige besides the tractor thing—we always pegged Tessa as the one to be more worried about—but I do know that she and Tessa have been best friends since forever."

I knew that, too, even though I was a transfer and hadn't come up with them like Audrey and Mariposa had. They always stuck together, even when they weren't doing student council stuff. They'd even campaigned together, even though most students ran solo and not on a single ticket.

"It would be a total betrayal," Audrey agreed. "There's a good chance Tessa doesn't have a clue what's going on."

"Well, lucky for her, this has become a matter of public concern," Mariposa said. "I don't really care about her, but anyone who thinks they can take out the president is too dangerous to leave standing. You find out what's going on, and if it's her, I'll take care of it. Permanently."

Then she ended the call and it kicked us all out. I wondered if she ever just said bye at the end of a conversation like a normal person, to spice things up.

Audrey and I spent the weekend coming up with our strategy for talking to Tessa. By Monday night when I went to bed, I felt pretty good.

Then, ten minutes later, I got up and pulled out the phone. There was still one last thing I needed to take care of.

CHAPTER FIFTEEN
POWER LUNCH

Tuesday after the long weekend, Audrey and I got to school early to meet Tessa in the library to interview her for the inaugural issue of the nonexistent *Fitz Herald*.

"You all good to go?" I confirmed with Audrey as we stood outside the library doors.

"Mm-hm," she said. "I have all my softball questions lined up, and then I can segue into the juicy stuff."

"Cool. Signal me if you need me to jump in. I got your back."

She knocked into my shoulder gently and smiled. "I know you do."

When we opened the door, Tessa was already there, supervising a banner that was being painted by two Space Cadet grunts. When she turned, I saw paint flecks were splattered across her face like extra freckles and realized that she must have helped paint it, too. Conor was right: She really did do the most.

She waved when she saw us and bounded over.

"DJ! Look at this. I was asking you questions last week, and now you're asking me. Weird, right?"

"Spooky," I agreed.

"Why didn't you tell me when we were talking? I didn't even know we had a school paper. And I know all the clubs."

"It's new," Audrey said smoothly, which wasn't technically a lie. "I'm Audrey, by the way."

"I know! You were in the school play. And I'm Tessa. Ha, you already know that, I bet."

"Full name is Contessa, right?" Audrey said. "That's what it said in the yearbook. Contessa McQueen."

Tessa snorted. "Yeah, but just call me Tessa in the article, OK? Contessa is already so extra. Contessa *McQueen*? I don't know what my parents were thinking."

"Isn't your sister's name Regina?" Audrey said, squinting.

"Mm-hm," she said, sounding like this was a path she'd gone down before.

"But Regina means 'queen.' So her name is—"

"Queen McQueen," Tessa finished. "Yup. This is what our parents did to us right out of the womb. Tragic."

"Prophetic," Audrey shot back. "Both of you ended up school presidents back-to-back."

"Ah, but we were democratically elected." She waved us over to a table, and we all sat down. "Is that what you want to talk about? The election?"

"Nah, that's old news," Audrey said. "We wanted to talk about the dance and the carnival."

Tessa perked up, which was impressive because she always seemed to be smiling and upbeat, like cameras were on her. "I'm really excited about the carnival! I mean, I'm excited about both, but the carnival was one of my initiatives."

"I heard they did one at the high school in December," I said. "It sounded like a lot of fun."

"Well," she said, "I don't know what they did at theirs, but ours is gonna be awesome. Lots of food, and a special surprise that I can't even tell you guys."

Audrey pouted. "Oh, come on. You can't even give us a teeny tiny little scoop?"

"Nope!" she said gleefully. "Oh, I will tell you this, though. It just got approved, and I'm super excited! You know how they're announcing candidates for Snow Prince and Princess later today?"

I nodded, even though I hadn't. I didn't even remember hearing anything about nominations since we'd come back, come to think about it, apart from Sienna's devoted fangirl.

"Well," Tessa continued, "we're going to have a dunk tank and a pieing station for the candidates at the carnival. Dunking for the boys, pieing for the girls. I mean, they have to agree, but I'm sure I can talk them into it. It'll be fun, right? Pied in the face today, crowned tomorrow. It's like symmetry or something. And it lets people know you're still down-to-earth, even if you're super popular. Plus, off the record, we all know Tyler's gonna be nominated, and if he does it, I bet the other three will follow his lead."

"Smart," said Audrey, which is what I was thinking, too. It's exactly how I would have handled the situation.

"Anyway," she said. "What questions do you have? Lay 'em on me. I'm an open book."

"Just some basic questions first," said Audrey. "You know, for your profile."

She nodded. "I got it; those are always first."

"Favorite color?"

"Light blue."

"Favorite book series?"

"A Series of Unfortunate Events! I love all the secret codes and all the mystery."

"Favorite food?"

"Ooh, tough one. I want to say my mom's mac and cheese, but also, I have never said no to pizza in my life."

They were safe and easy questions. Priming questions to make her more receptive to more prying ones.

"Why did you decide to run for president?" Audrey said, inching closer to the actual topic at hand like a Venus flytrap slowly closing. "'Cause of your sister?"

Tessa rolled her eyes, but not in a way that made it seem like it was directed at Audrey. More at the world in general. "Everyone always thinks that, and it wasn't even her idea to run in the first place! Like, yeah, I was vice president before, so it was kind of natural, but I really just wanted to help people, you know? Make a difference." Then she kind of snorted. "OK, that sounds cheesy. I know school president isn't like actual president. I'm not saving the planet or anything. But, like, the canned food drive? They didn't have that before. That was me. And the carnival, that was my idea, even before the high school did it. Ours got postponed because of the snow, but I thought of it first. I just want things to be as good as I can make them, you know?"

I nodded without meaning to. She was so earnest: That was how she'd won the election. You could tell she meant what she said. That it was more than just winning a popularity contest for her. Which is why it was so important to keep her safe if Paige was planning something shady. And speaking of Paige . . .

"What about Paige?" Audrey said. "Did she want all that, too, or did you have to talk her into running? Not a lot of people ran together like you two did."

Tessa laughed. "Oh, I didn't have to talk her into anything. We do everything together! From when we were little. Sleepovers, Halloween costumes. Oh! We used to write each other secret messages in class with those Starcade invisible-ink pens."

Her eyes went fuzzy with warmth. "We met when we were both in kindergarten. Her family was having this fall festival thing for the community on their farm. We played with the goats, and then she took me up to her house and we had the best cookies." It looked like she could still taste those cookies in her mind. "We've been best friends ever since."

"Aww, cute!" Audrey said. "How has working together been?"

"Great," said Tessa. "We get to plan out stuff together, and she has a lot of great ideas. And this is gonna look so good on our résumés. It helps people, it looks good for us, and I get to do it with my BFF? Win, win, win, right?"

"Right," said Audrey. "So, there haven't been any problems? I know people sometimes have problems when they work with their friends. Especially when you have to boss them around. Like, I had this class project one time with one of my choir friends. Love her, but she could not stand me telling her what to do. We had to switch groups to save the friendship."

"No, nothing like that," said Tessa. "I don't boss her around. And she doesn't boss me around."

"Does she feel like you do, though?" Audrey prodded.

Tessa frowned. "No. She'd tell me if I was doing anything that annoyed her. That's a weird question—why are you asking?"

"Just following up on a tip," Audrey said smoothly. "We assumed it was bogus, but we had to follow up."

"I don't know who said that we were having problems, but they must just be trying to start something," she said, sounding like she was offended we'd even bring it up. "The dance is next week on Saturday, and things are already crazy because it was postponed. I don't have the brain space to deal with this, too."

"Don't worry," Audrey said. "It won't be in the article. I just had to say I asked." She rolled her eyes playfully like they were good friends. "People always wanna assume just 'cause two girls are friends there has to be drama, right?"

"Yeah!" Tessa said, brightening. "It's so annoying!" And boom, she was back on our side.

Audrey finished off the interview without turning the conversation back to Paige, and I snapped some pics of Tessa and the banner for our "article." Then we met Mariposa and the others in the conference room in the front office, this time without a full breakfast buffet.

"She doesn't know anything about Paige," Audrey said. "Either that or she's fooling herself and she doesn't want to know. I saw it in her eyes: She doesn't believe Paige would ever do anything like that to her. She means it."

"Do you think she's right?" Conor asked.

Audrey shrugged. "I mean, like I said, they've been BFFs forever. Tessa would know her really well. But also, people change."

"I still think Paige is suspect," said Mariposa. "But even if it's not her, Tessa is still a huge target, especially so close to her two biggest events of the year. If someone wants to ruin her, now is the time."

"I think you're right," I said. "Based on the note they left you, this isn't just practical, this is personal. The BPS has a mission, and Tessa would be the biggest symbolic target. But she's probably not gonna be on the lookout for threats. She doesn't have any reason to believe anything is wrong, and she's smart but she's so busy."

"She *is* surrounded by Space Cadets a lot," Audrey said. "That's *some* protection at least."

Mariposa sneered. "Please. The pretend cops with their pretend badges? They're useless."

Monty frowned. "I'm a Space Cadet."

"Oh, there's no way that's legit. I know that was part of

some scheme. You're a pretend Space Cadet, which makes you pretend useless."

I wasn't sure if she meant it as a compliment or not, but, either way, Monty brightened.

"Oh! I almost forgot," he said. "Here's your butterfly."

She took it from him, totally deadpan, but when she moved to shove it in her front pocket, she hesitated and then carefully slid it into her back pocket instead. I shot Audrey a look to make sure we'd seen the same thing before returning to the conversation.

"We can use the Space Cadet thing to our advantage," I said. "Monty, you're in good with Caro. Try to get on dance duty. Tessa usually has a couple of Space Cadets helping her out. If anything seems fishy, shut it down."

The bell rang, and we all split up to get to our classes.

"See you later," I said to Audrey as I turned to go to homeroom.

"Yeah, after school, right?"

I grinned, but I didn't answer.

A couple of hours later, in the middle of my lunch period, there was an urgent problem with Audrey's records, which meant she had to get to the front office right away.

When she saw me waiting in the office, she realized "records problem" must be code for something else, and she slipped into game face.

"What's going on?" she whispered as I led her to the conference room. "Did Monty find something? Is Tessa OK? What do you need me to— Oh."

Instead of a war room with the whole gang, it was just me and the best spread I could manage on a night's notice, which wasn't too shabby. Her fave sandwiches that I'd made that night at home, contraband Cherry Cokes I'd gotten through one of Conor's hookups, the fancy kettle chips that she liked that they only had in the teachers' lounge vending machines, and ice cream from the cafeteria I'd picked up on the way here.

She gasped. "Oh my gosh, where are the others? Is this all for me?"

"Surprise," I said, spreading a hand above the table. "I know we're in the middle of this big thing right now, but last night I called Mariposa and had her pull some strings. The guys helped, too."

"I can see that," she said, picking up the origami rose on the table, courtesy of Monty. "What's it all for?"

"Well, we never get to have lunch together," I said, pulling out her chair.

"Not your fault," she said as she sat. "We have different lunch periods."

"Yeah, but we never hang out at school at all," I said. "That's my fault."

She kind of shrugged and picked at the chipped polish on her nails. "I know it's for the good of the team, but—"

I shook my head. "It wasn't just that. I was worried about you, too. You can be mad if you want; I deserve it. I know you can handle yourself. It's not that I don't trust you or believe in you. Or that I don't want you around! I never want you to think that I don't need you. *Never.* It just makes me antsy sometimes. But that's my problem, not yours. And I'm sorry for being kinda controlling. I shouldn't have done that."

"You shouldn't have," she agreed. But she didn't sound like she was mad at me. More like she was happy I'd finally admitted it.

She reached across the table and touched my shoulder. "And, DJ, if you feel weird, that *is* my problem. We can do baby steps, you know? And come up with a reason we'd be hanging out. Like, now we're on the 'school paper' together. That's a great cover. Sidenote, do we actually have to do that now? Like, write a school paper? Because I'll do it; I just need to know."

"Possibly? I need to check with Mariposa."

"Oh! Mariposa. I wanted to ask, why did she do this? She's not in the business of giving away favors for free. What did she ask for?"

"Nothing," I said.

"Nothing," Audrey repeated dubiously. "That... doesn't sound like her. Maybe she's trying to get us on her good side so she can use us later?"

"Maybe that's part of it," I said. "But... she knew about you. From Duke's Starcade recordings. She knew about us. I think she might just, I dunno, like us?"

Audrey smiled. "I like us, too." Then she gasped and grabbed the can of soda in front of her. "I just had a great idea. We can make floats with the ice cream!"

I was going to agree that it was a fantastic idea and she could take over for me as Brains anytime, when the intercom suddenly crackled on.

"Attention, students." It was the principal. "I know you've all been waiting, and now it's time for us to announce the nominees for Snow Prince and Princess. First up, for prince, we have Dylan Carter and Tyler Monroe."

At Tyler's name, Audrey did her best fake-shocked face, and I cracked up.

"And for the girls, Sienna Chase and Paige Tran."

Audrey's eyes met mine immediately.

"Wait," she said. "Did they just say . . . ?"

"Voting is open online from now until Thursday at midnight. Good luck to all our nominees!" The intercom went silent.

"Paige," I said. "Paige is in the running for princess. That's . . . that's weird. I mean, I guess Tessa is popular. They're BFFs, so if she campaigned for her, then maybe she could get the nom, but—" I shook my head. Logistics weren't the issue here. "Wait. Back to what we were saying before. Do you remember?"

She nodded like she was sitting right next to me on this train of thought. "Yeah! If Paige is the mastermind but Tessa isn't the target . . ." Audrey started.

"Then maybe it's Sienna," I finished. "I mean, we don't

know anything for sure, but if I were Sienna, and I knew what we knew, I'd be worried."

"We should tell Mariposa," Audrey said. "Right away, if we can. Sienna will need a full protection detail, not just Monty. We don't have the manpower for that."

"Already dialing," I said, pulling out my phone.

Mariposa had told us to call her right away if anything came up. I trusted that she had a way to answer without getting in trouble.

As soon as she picked up, I started talking. "Mariposa! It's not Tessa. She's not the target. It's—"

"Sienna," she said.

"Yeah. You heard the announcement."

"No. I mean, I did, but that's not how I know."

"Then how?"

"I just got contacted by the BPS," Mariposa said. "They want me to rocket boost her."

CHAPTER SIXTEEN
MEDIA BLACKOUT

I texted Conor to ditch lunch, and Monty got out on a fake Space Cadet call generated by Mariposa so we could all talk in the conference room. This wasn't a later problem. This was a now problem. I knew from experience how quickly rocket boostings happened. The only reason it wouldn't be expected today was because the morning announcements had already happened. We had to figure out a way to stop it.

Or that's what I thought at least.

"OK, so we rocket boost her," Mariposa said with a shrug. "I can authorize those. And even if I couldn't, they'd assume the order was from Lucky."

"Wha— No!" I said. Is that why she thought I'd called an all-hands-on-deck meeting? "We can't just rocket boost her!"

"Oh," said Mariposa. "Are one of you friends with her or something?"

"Not really, no," I said. We'd helped her out when she was in trouble, but I wouldn't call us friends.

She squinted at me. "Then you owe her a favor."

"No." If anything, she owed us one.

"Then why can't I rocket boost her?"

"Because she hasn't done anything to deserve it!" I said. "Why am I explaining to you that rocket boosting people is bad? You know that! That's why you do it!"

She shrugged. "Collateral damage. I'm in the BPS officially. I can't say no without a good reason, or they'll realize I'm playing with them, and it'll ruin our chance at getting any more inside information. Not worth it. Better to just let one random person go down so we can get to the bottom of this and stop them than to have them suss me out and blow this whole operation."

Audrey and I exchanged a glance. Mariposa might have let us have the conference room for lunch with no strings attached, but this was still Mariposa without a doubt. She hadn't gone soft.

"Ehh, she's got a point, guys," Conor said, swiping half my sandwich off my plate. I didn't even try to stop him.

"Conor!" Audrey said, sounding outraged. "We literally robbed a Starcade last year so you wouldn't get rocket boosted. You're gonna let it happen to someone else?"

"I'm not for it," he said, "but if the only other option is Mariposa getting busted, then I feel like we're kinda stuck here."

"Was not expecting him to be the voice of reason here, but he's right," Mariposa said.

"Insulting and complimentary all rolled into one," Conor said. "Impressive." He reached for my ice cream cup, too, but I batted his hand away. I had my limits.

"Mariposa," I said firmly. "This isn't what we do."

"Well, then it's a good thing you don't have to," she said easily. "I'll take care of it."

"We can't let you do it, either," I said.

She scoffed. "You won't *let* me? What are you gonna do? Sic Monty on me?"

Monty gasped. "What? No! Mariposa, I wouldn't do that!"

That seemed to fluster her a bit. "No, I know you

wouldn't—I was just making a— Monty, I was being rhetorical."

"Oh, good." He smiled.

Then Audrey smiled.

"Hey, Monty," she said. "You haven't given your opinion yet. What do you think about rocket boosting Sienna?"

"Do we have to?" he said. "I know I don't make the plans, but it seems mean."

"I agree," I said, picking up on what she was doing. "That's a great point, Monty. It would be mean. Mariposa, do you disagree with Monty?"

She looked as close to stricken as a person could look without actually moving their face at all.

"I'm not saying it's not mean," she said. "I'm saying we don't have a choice. I don't rocket boost people because it's fun for me. I do it because it's the best move."

"What if we could come up with a better one?" I said.

"By the end of the school day?" she said dubiously.

"I figured out how to raise one hundred thousand Starcade tickets in two weeks," I said. "I think that should get me a little faith."

She seemed to consider that. "If you can figure it out by the end of the day, fine. But otherwise, I'm doing it, and you can figure out how you feel about it after." Without giving us another second to argue, she swept out of the room.

"Seriously, dude?" I said to Conor once I was sure she was gone.

"What?" he said. "You pulled me out of lunch! I'm hungry!"

"No, not that! Although yeah, also that! But mostly, what happened to our united front? You can't just agree with her when she says something like that!"

"Hey, I didn't say it was gonna get us into the Scouting Hall of Fame. I just said it was a rock/hard place situation. Which it is."

"But we can find another way, right?" said Monty. "It's what we do."

"It is," I agreed. "But we don't have a lot of time."

"Why don't you just interrupt the announcements again," said Conor. "It worked to stop mine."

"It did, but we only had to stop it for one day. Here, we need to stop it every day until the dance happens. If we have the alarm go off every day, then it's gonna be obvious that something is up."

"And they'll be able to trace it back to us more easily if we pay off people to do it with tickets, like you did with Duke last semester."

"Exactly," I said. "But I like the general idea. If we take out the announcements, that's a system breakdown that's not Mariposa's fault, and it'll have to be postponed until after they're back on again."

"We could sabotage the AV equipment," Conor offered. "Steal some wires. Wipe some files. Temporarily, of course."

Back at my old school I would have green-lit that plan right away, but now, unlike Mariposa, I was trying to avoid collateral damage if possible.

"Let's save that for plan B," I said. "I'm wondering if there's a more low-impact way we can handle this."

"What if we talk to someone who works on the announcements?" asked Monty. "Audrey, you have friends in the AV department, right? Didn't some of them help with the show last year?"

"He's right," said Audrey. "I'm pretty close with a couple of them. They tend to help with the lighting and effects and striking the set after the shows. But I don't know how bribable any of them are."

"We don't want to leave a trail anyway," I said. "Or count on outsiders to lie for us. But," I said, gears starting to turn in my head, "we don't have to convince our target to shut down the announcements if they come up with the idea themselves."

"You wanna try a Shoulder Devil?" asked Conor.

"Exactly." I checked the clock. There were twenty minutes left in lunch. I turned to Audrey. "Wanna finish up here and then do some fake reporting?"

"Sounds fun!" she said. "I like doing the Lois Lane/Clark Kent thing."

"OK," I said. "We'll try to figure this out, and if we can't, Conor, you can do your thing. In the meantime, see what you can find out about Sienna."

"Aye, aye," said Conor. "Let's go, Monty. Enjoy your lunch date."

"Lunch da—?" I started, but Conor darted off, grabbing a chip from my bag as he went.

"Bye, guys!" Monty said cheerfully, leaving and closing the door behind him.

I turned to Audrey quickly for damage control. "Sorry about all that. And ignore Conor. He's being an idiot."

"Is he?" she said, popping the tab of her soda and pouring it into her ice cream cup.

She couldn't tell, but my cheeks felt as red as the cherry in her Coke.

Ten minutes later, we were on our way to the AV classroom, plan worked out over sandwiches and Coke floats.

When we opened the door, we saw that kids were already separated into groups working on laptops and playing with camera equipment.

Mr. Drucker was sitting at his desk, eating a powdered doughnut and flipping through the newspaper.

"Hi, Mr. Drucker," Audrey said. "I'm here for—"

He just nodded and waved her forward with sugar-dusted hands. She shot me a glance and shrugged. Sometimes you come up with an airtight cover story and the person it's for just wants to eat a doughnut in peace. Take the win.

Audrey scanned the room, then subtly nodded to the far corner. "Ah, good. Stephanie. I know her."

Stephanie was a small girl, with light brown skin and black hair that settled around her shoulders in loose waves.

"Hey, Steph!" Audrey called, waving as we approached her.

Stephanie looked up, said something to the team she was working with, then came to greet us.

"Hey, Audrey," she said, squinting, a bit confused. "And DJ, right? Flounder from the show?"

"DJ from the school paper now," said Audrey.

"We have a school paper?" said Stephanie.

"We do now!" Audrey answered.

"Why am I just hearing about this?" Stephanie said, whipping out a notebook and pen with lightning speed. "You should be partnering with the school news. Obvious synergy there."

"That's why we came," Audrey said. "To talk to you about that."

"Yeah," I chimed in. "Everyone knows you do all the work anyway. You and your team. You guys handle all the equipment, right? The cameras and the audio and all that."

She nodded proudly. "Plus, the green screens for weather and all of the transcripts."

"Wow," said Audrey. "That's so much. What's left for the anchors to do?"

She shrugged. "They read the news, I guess."

"Do they memorize it?" I asked.

"No," she said. "They read it off a teleprompter, like on the actual news."

"And you guys run the teleprompter?" asked Audrey.

"It's part of the *V* of *AV*," she said. "So yeah."

"Well, I'm sure they write the news, then, right? Like we're gonna. They write the scripts and then get approval?"

"They . . ." She stopped and thought for a second. "No, I don't think they do, actually. I think the segments are mostly prewritten by other kids and they just put them in order."

"Huh, weird," said Audrey. She shrugged. "Well, anyway, we also wanted to ask you how you do the credits for everyone. We'll need to do credits for the paper, and we thought it'd be easiest to just do the same thing as you. But the credits roll kinda fast, so we thought we'd ask to be sure. It's just in alphabetical order, right? To be fair?"

"No, it's the anchors first, then us."

"Why?" asked Audrey.

"I . . . I guess because they're more recognizable. When you think about the announcements, you think about them, not us."

"Isn't that more reason to have your names first? I mean, you're doing so much work and it's all behind the scenes."

"It's not that big a . . . deal," she said, but it was clear from the shake in her voice that she wasn't quite sure she believed that.

"Still," said Audrey. "Maybe you should talk to them about having it changed? It's only fair. Or you should—"

"Strike!" I said, snapping my fingers.

"What?" said Audrey and Stephanie at once.

"Sorry, not you," I said to Stephanie. I turned to Audrey. "You said you needed people to strike the set for the next show. You know, taking down all the set pieces and stuff. Do you think we could put an announcement in the paper?"

"Oh, good idea," she said. "Lemme make a note." She pulled out a notebook and started writing. "We also need to pick the movie we're reviewing for the movie review column. What were the options?"

"There's that new superhero movie, that one with the talking dogs, and . . . hmm. There was a third one, but I don't remember the name. It's that old musical. Umm, about the newspaper guys in New York and they decide to stop working 'cause they're not being treated fairly. What's it called again?"

"*Newsies!*" Audrey said, clapping her hands together excitedly. "We watched it at the wrap party last year, remember, Steph?"

"Hmm? Right, yeah, I remember."

I could see the gears in her head start turning. Audrey flashed me a quick look that said, *Hooked her*, and then said, "OK, just wanted to get your opinions. Let's stay in touch—you have my number, right? I think partnering up is a good idea. And if you ever need anything announced, let us know."

"I might take you up on that."

Five minutes before school ended, I got a text from Audrey. It was a screenshot of a conversation with Stephanie.

Do you have access to the school printer for the paper? I need to get some flyers printed FAST.

It looked like the strike was on. The rocket boosting was off. We had our chance. Now, we just needed to make the most of it.

CHAPTER SEVENTEEN
AND YOUR ENEMIES CLOSER

We met up with Mariposa the next morning, and she confirmed that our plan had gone off as intended. Kinda hard to rocket boost someone when the announcements are temporarily suspended due to the entire AV team learning about picket lines through the power of twenty-year-olds dressed as newspaper boys who sing and dance.

"The BPS left me a message in my locker calling off the hit," Mariposa said. "But this will only slow them down. We have to figure this out as quickly as possible."

"I'll start thinking of a plan," I said. The more we learned, the more nervous I got about knocking over this house of cards. There was way more structure to this organization than any other I'd ever tangled with. I had no idea what might happen if we came in like a wrecking ball. Precision was key if we didn't want to be left playing a very messy game of fifty-two-card pickup when this was over.

Mariposa pulled a slip of paper from her pocket and held it out to me.

"They also sent me this."

I scanned it over. It was a note, directing her to vote for Paige and get everyone who was scared of her to do the same.

"Well," I said. "That confirms it. Gotta be her. Who else would want her to be Snow Princess this bad?"

"I'm surprised she'd want it herself, though," Audrey said. "She's never really been into any of that stuff. I guess she could have been secretly jealous this whole time but didn't feel like she could go for it until now, since she's VP and all."

"Sometimes people snap," Mariposa said simply. "I've seen it happen."

"Well, let's try to nip it in the bud. This dance already got snowed out. We don't want it sabotaged, too. Conor, can you fill Mariposa in on what we learned about Sienna when we looked into her earlier?"

"Right, Sienna Chase," he said. "She's an eighth

grader. Wasn't hard to find her online because, well, she is extremely online." He flashed us screenshots from several social media profiles. In each pic she was stylishly dressed, with perfect makeup and a hairstyle to match. "All her pictures are like this. And she's been vlogging her entire Snow Princess campaign. She's already one of the most popular girls in school, so you'd think she'd be a shoo-in, but she's also been campaigning the most."

"She treats this like it's her job," Mariposa murmured under her breath.

"You're not wrong," Conor said. "I mean, look at this stuff." He pulled up videos and showed us snippets from the most recent—surprising her little sister with a WELCOME HOME display after her successful surgery, a rant video about the absolute *worst* math teacher at school, a story-time video about how a bee attacked her at the park and she *literally* almost died. "There are effects and text overlays and she's constantly posting. Lots of kids have channels they mess around on, but she's, like, putting real effort into this. I think she wants to get free stuff from companies when she's in high school. Brand deals and stuff."

"Makes sense she would throw her hat in the ring here, then," I said. "Kind of like an influencer test run."

"I still think it would have been easier to rocket boost her," said Mariposa. "Then we wouldn't have to be on guard for another big thing right now."

"No," I said firmly. "She's not one of our friends, but she doesn't deserve that just for existing and trying to be popular. That's not a crime."

Mariposa shrugged. "Whatever you say, but I'm not here to bodyguard middle school Barbie. Anything else happens to her? That's your problem."

"But she won't have any protection," Monty said, looking like he'd just gotten blindsided by one of those sad puppy-adoption commercials. "We have to help her!"

"We really don't," Mariposa said, but there was a flash of weakness in her eyes, the same kind I can spot in my mom's eyes when I know I'm one "Please?" away from pizza for dinner.

"Mariposa," he said, drawing out the syllables, and she sighed.

I suppressed a smile deep down inside. Monty strikes again.

"Fine. I'll see what I can do. But if I'm wasting my time on this, you all better double down on Paige."

"Can't we just call off the strike and rocket boost her?" Conor said. "Or is she off-limits, too?"

"Even if we could right now, it wouldn't be smart," said Mariposa.

"Agreed," I said, making a mental note to make sure Mariposa wasn't rubbing off on Conor too much. "If we do this in a sloppy way, there could be unintended consequences. Remember, we're trying to limit collateral damage here."

"And we should try to figure out what she's planning on doing to Sienna," Audrey pointed out. "Like you guys said, she'll just try something else, and there are still a lot of nasty things you can do to a kid besides rocket boosting them. She might already have something planned. I know we need to talk to Paige, but maybe we should also talk to Sienna. You know, cover our bases. See if she's noticed anything weird."

"You two could do the newspaper thing again," Conor suggested. "I don't think Sienna is gonna say no to having her picture taken."

"My thoughts exactly," I said. "We can figure out a time to do that today. And when we talked to Tessa, she said that there's still prep going on for the carnival after school. We should volunteer. Talk to Paige. Scout the scene and see if anything jumps out."

Audrey grimaced slightly. "That sounds like a good idea, but I have a dentist's appointment after school."

"Don't worry, Auds," Conor said. "We can handle things without you for one day."

"Just focus on Sienna," I agreed. "We'll handle Paige."

Audrey and Sienna had the same lunch period, so we decided that was the best time to strike. As anticipated, Sienna had no questions about a feature story all about her, except for which filters we planned to use for her photo in the paper.

"Obviously, you can't do anything wild like dog ears, but a tasteful pastel filter—or maybe go the opposite and do a lo-fi filter so everything really pops. Depends on the outfit. How many outfit changes do I get? I wish you'd warned me about this so I could have gotten dressed up."

Sienna sat across from us in the library, hair in perfect waves, expensive-looking top paired with expensive-looking jeans, eyeliner sharp enough to stab someone with. And this was just for a normal day of school. I was fascinated to see how she thought she was going to escalate from there, but Audrey said, "That's, like, totally our bad, but this was so short notice. I have an idea. What if you send us some pictures that you've taken and we can use one of those?"

The tension in Sienna's body melted away. "Yes! That's perfect, thank you!" She smiled like we'd just told her we'd gotten her the kidney transplant she needed. "People always get so aggro when I suggest that, but it's, like, I'm doing your job for you. Why are you getting upset? And do you really think you can take a better picture of me than me? Trust me, I have way more practice."

"I bet," I said.

"You're a total pro," Audrey gushed. "I've seen the pics you post, and they're all mega cute. You must put a lot of work into them."

Sienna beamed. "Ohmigosh, thank you! You totally get me. My parents are always all, like, 'You spend too much time on your phone,' but I'm like 'Hello, guys, I'm building a brand. That doesn't just happen.' Can you believe they have me on a limited data plan? Like, I'm doing my best here, but they're making it so annoying."

"Parents," Audrey said with an eye roll.

"Totally," Sienna agreed. "Hey. Do you think you can talk to the yearbook committee? I was having a"—she lowered her voice—"*challenging hair day* on picture day, so I didn't come to school, and they won't let me get a redo or submit my own pics."

"We'll see what we can do," Audrey said smoothly, "but hey! Congrats on your nomination!"

Sienna put one hand on her heart and another out like she was gesturing to an imaginary audience to stop with the applause already because it was too much for her to take.

"I know, I know. I can't say it was actually a surprise, but it's still *totally* an honor."

"*Totally* not a surprise," Audrey said, mirroring back her pronunciation of the word. I loved watching her work so much. "I gotta be honest, though, I was a little surprised to hear about Paige."

"Who?" said Sienna. "Oh! Right, Tractor Tran. Yeah, that was . . . weird." She opened and closed her perfectly glossed lips like she was trying to decide whether she should say something.

I glanced over at Audrey and tilted my head slightly upward. *Get it out of her.*

"She doesn't have anything close to your numbers on any socials," Audrey said. "I mean, the math doesn't really add up."

"I know, right?" Sienna said, indecision swiftly broken. "How'd she get the nomination? Like, she has Tessa in her corner, sure, but it's not like she was campaigning for her. How would she have the time?"

Sienna looked to the left and to the right and motioned for us to lean closer.

"I wasn't going to say this," she whispered, "because it sounds a little 'tinfoil hat,' you know?"

We are way past that, I thought.

"But I'm a little suspicious," Sienna continued. "About the nominations. They started last semester, before the storm. I had all the votes I needed to qualify for the final vote. But then, after it got snowed out, some of the records were lost, so they decided to hold noms again to make it fair."

I frowned. "I don't remember them announcing that." Sure, I'd been avoiding dance news, but I'd been avoiding it last semester, too, and it hadn't helped much. Come to think of it, it was strange that Sienna was the only person I'd seen campaign flyers from since we'd come back for break.

"I know," said Sienna. "I only found out about it because I went to the front desk to ask about the tiara's color palette so I can make sure my outfit doesn't clash for when I win. But I bet there are people who didn't realize they were redoing voting for nominations and got knocked out because they thought they already had enough nominations. And who's in charge of dance stuff? Student government."

Audrey and I looked at each other. I didn't know that they were just letting kids be fully in charge of the dance like that, but they definitely had influence. Tessa had planned a lot on her own, suggesting the food drive and talking to outside companies. It wasn't a total stretch that Paige could suggest a little change to the nomination rules and be taken seriously. And I knew for a fact that Lucky and Mariposa had sway over what was read on the morning announcements. Heck, we'd gotten them shut down completely. It would be just as easy for Paige to make sure the little detail of do-over nominations wasn't broadly announced, and with everyone busy with makeup work after the snowstorm, it could get lost in the shuffle.

"But you didn't hear it from me," Sienna said, moving out of the whisper zone. She stopped. "Unless you're going to make this a whole investigative thing? Like one of those murder-mystery podcasts. Then you have to have me on board. I'd be great on a podcast. Those are great for engagement. Are we friends on all the socials? We should get in touch."

We promised Sienna we'd get in touch if we were considering a podcast and sent her back to lunch so we could talk.

"That was more info than I expected," Audrey said.

"People care about what they care about," I said. "If you wanna find the conspiracy theory in winter formal nominations, talk to the popular girl."

"Does this help us, though?" Audrey asked. "We already knew Paige was willing to break rules to get what she wants. So she rigged the nominations. Big deal. That doesn't tell us what she's going to do next."

"Maybe not," I said. "But we can use it as evidence when we take her down. If we're not rocket boosting her, we might have to get the actual authorities involved." I hated bringing in teachers as much as the next guy, but sometimes there weren't any other options.

"I know Mariposa said she'd watch out for her, but I might stick around her, too," Audrey said. "Couldn't hurt to have the extra eyes, and she said she'd—"

Her phone buzzed in her pocket and then, a second later, so did mine. I checked. A friend request from Sienna.

"Ha," said Audrey. "Looks like I'm already in."

"Me too."

The second I accepted the request, typing dots appeared followed by a message.

> *Let me know if you and Audrey ever wanna be in a vlog. You'd make **such** a cute couple!* ♥

I quickly turned off my screen and shoved my phone in my pocket. If Audrey had gotten a similar message from her, she didn't show it. I cleared my throat and got back on topic.

"Good idea, sticking to Sienna," I said. "Let me know if you find anything suspicious. In the meantime, I have to figure out what I'm going to say to Paige later today. I'm filling in for you. Big shoes."

She giggled. "Don't worry. You'll do great. You're gonna wanna drop her guard. Get her to talk about stuff she likes. The way I did with Tessa. Like her farm. I remember I sat next to her on the bus for a field trip in fifth grade and she talked about her cows for like forty-five minutes straight."

"Sounds like a plan," I said. "Have fun getting your teeth scraped."

"Gross! I'll talk to you later!"

I filled the boys in on what we'd learned and, a few hours later, we were standing outside the gym, ready for our second mission of the day.

"I'll be checking my phone," I said. "Don't be obvious, but if you hear anything suspicious, let me know."

Conor nodded. "We should go in separately so no one knows we're together."

"Right," I said. "Monty first, since they're expecting him as a cadet. Then me, then you. We'll meet up and talk after."

After we sent Monty in, I took a second to get my game face on (which in this case didn't look much like a game face, but that's sometimes the best move) and then walked into the room.

It looked like Santa's workshop in the offseason. Lots of kids in little groups painting banners and cutting snowflake decorations. In the back of the room, I spotted Caro barking orders at Monty and Santiago, who caught my gaze and rolled his eyes like *Can you believe this?* I couldn't blame him. At the center of the room, organizing the chaos, was Tessa, who waved me over when she spotted me.

"DJ!" she said. "I wasn't expecting you. Did you need more for your story?" She looked around. "Where's Audrey?"

"At the dentist," I said. "And no, I just came to help out. You mentioned during the interview that you could use volunteers, so here I am, volunteering."

"Oh! That's great!" She scanned the room. "Hmm, let's see. We can always use more people on snowflakes if you're good with scissors. Or you can help with stuffing the goodie bags or wrapping the raffle prizes or painting the banners."

I scrunched up my face like I was deliberating, but I

already knew where I wanted to go. "I'm pretty good with a pair of scissors," I said. "I can do snowflakes."

"Awesome," she said. "We need a bunch. Oh, and that's where Paige is!"

"Oh, is she?" I said as if I didn't already absolutely know.

"Yeah, you can get set up with her. She'll tell you what to do." The door behind me opened, and Conor walked in. "Oh, I think that's another volunteer! The turnout has been fantastic. I really think this carnival is gonna go great!"

"I hope so," I said under my breath. I walked over to the snowflake station, giving Paige a thorough once-over as I did. She was wearing a pullover sweater with a little sheep embroidered onto it.

Tessa had said she was running the station, but unlike Tessa, who always seemed like she was taking charge of whatever room she was in, Paige was just sitting, putting all her concentration into the one snowflake she was cutting. Vice president and stuck on snowflake duty. I wondered for a second if Paige didn't have some secret beef with Tessa, but tossed the thought. If Audrey thought they were fine, then so did I. Still, it seemed like the exact kind of thing that would build up and up until you had to send that angry energy somewhere—maybe not at your best friend, but that left future web influencer Sienna wide open.

"Hey!" I said as I approached, trying for friendly and casual. I don't know which I failed at, but she jumped.

"Sorry," I said, trying to get things back to even. Jumpy wasn't a good baseline if I wanted her comfortable enough to start spilling things. But maybe her jumpiness was because she was hiding some pretty incriminating extracurricular activities. I filed that away for later. "I was just looking for—"

"Tess is over there," she said, pointing back to where she was now talking to Conor.

"Oh, no," I said. "I was just talking to her. I was actually looking for you."

She properly looked up from her snowflake for the first time. "Me? Why?"

I pointed down at the snowflake she was cutting, and she hit herself on the forehead, narrowly missing poking herself with the scissors. I winced.

"Oh, duh," she said. "Here, let me get you set up. You'll need paper and scissors and, oh, here's a pattern. These have the triangle-point ones. I like the triangle-point ones."

I took the items as she handed them over and sat across from her at the little table that was set up. I kinda paused to see if she'd give me any more direction, but she didn't. She was going right back into her bubble, which was exactly what I didn't want. Clearly conversation starting wasn't her thing. That was OK; she didn't have to start it.

"So," I said as I carefully lined up the pattern on my folded piece of paper. This was a cover, but I didn't want to play a part in ruining the dance that was already in jeopardy with my sloppy decoration making. "I don't know if you know this, but I'm with the newspaper."

"We have a newspaper?"

"We do now," I said, mentally reminding myself to figure out if there was a way we could get away with not writing this paper we'd used as an excuse to several people now and that was officially on the books as a club with funding. "We're doing profiles on kids in student government. I came to volunteer, not ask questions, but I figured, two birds and all."

She shrugged. "Yeah, I can answer."

"Great. Favorite book?"

"*Charlotte's Web*. Tess likes the Series of Unfortunate Events series."

"Favorite subject?"

"Gym, I guess. Tess likes French best."

"Favorite color?"

"Green. Tess's is blue, but, like, only light blue."

I paused. I hadn't even asked about Tessa's answers, and she was volunteering them up like it was a given that that's what I really wanted. It sounded like she was used to playing second fiddle. The exact kind of person who would start something like the BPS. Still, I wanted her to talk less about Tessa, more about herself, so I switched gears.

"What about the dance? I heard you're up for Snow Princess. That's pretty cool."

She shrugged. "It's whatever, I guess."

She was hiding something. I wasn't sure what, and I wished Audrey was around to fish it out of her, but even I could tell that wasn't the full story.

"'Whatever'?" I prodded. "That's it? I mean, it's you and Sienna! That's a pretty big deal."

She snorted. "Me and Sienna. It doesn't feel like we should be in the same sentence, let alone the same competition. You know I didn't even vote?"

"No?" I said, thinking about the conversation with Sienna.

"No. I don't really pay attention to that stuff."

I nodded neutrally, but inside I was thinking, *Laying it on a little thick, huh?* But it made sense. I was, allegedly, putting this info in the (still imaginary) school paper. Anything to make her seem not involved was good—at least to someone who wasn't looking too deeply into everything she was saying. If she was running a school-wide conspiracy under everyone's noses, I had to assume she could convincingly play dumb, too.

"I honestly thought it was some kind of joke at first," she said. "You know, like Carrie on prom night? But Tess checked the nominations and she said it's legit." She lowered her voice. "I think she just told everyone who was gonna vote for her to vote for me instead, since she wasn't eligible. You know, 'cause she was running the whole thing."

She was distancing herself from the process. Throwing Tessa under the bus? But Audrey had been pretty sure their closeness was real. Well, Tessa's read on their closeness anyway. She seemed determined to keep bringing up Tessa, so I decided to follow Audrey's advice and go with that.

"You and Tessa are pretty close, right?"

"Yeah!" she said. "We've been friends since . . . since . . . oh! We had this petting zoo at my farm a long time ago. There were a lot of kids from our school, but no one really wanted to hang out with me. I was wandering around, and I saw her by the goat pen. She wanted to see the horses, but her sister wanted to see the goats, so they were stuck there. She was all pouty, so I helped her sneak some goat feed into her sister's back pocket, and the goats were biting her butt the entire time she was in the pen. It was hilarious. And we've been BFFs ever since."

It was a funny story, but more important, finally a flicker of the kind of thinking that ended up with you as the head of a secret revenge society.

I made small talk with her for a little longer as we cut snowflakes, and eventually, it was time to go. I met up with Conor and Monty in the hall.

"I didn't notice anything weird going on," said Monty. "You were with Paige the whole time, and I didn't see anyone else doing anything suspicious."

"And I didn't see any obvious sabotage," said Conor. "Like, I thought maybe the dunk tank, but they're both going to get dunked so—"

"Wait," I said, stopping him. "Dunk tank? I thought it was boys getting dunked, girls getting pied."

"That's not what Tessa said to me. She said girls are being dunked, boys are getting pied."

I frowned. "Give me one second." I ducked back in and beelined for Tessa, who was packing up some supplies. "Hey, Tessa?"

"Huh? Oh, DJ! What's up?"

"Quick question for the article. Did you say boys dunked, girls pied?"

"Oh, no," she said. "We changed it. Girls are doing the dunk tank, boys are doing the pie booth. We figured longer hair, whipped cream? Bleh."

We? "You and Paige decided?"

"Yeah. Of course."

"Cool, thanks." I headed back to the guys. That was a plausible reason to swap. It could be nothing. Or it could be a setup.

"Last-minute swap," I announced. "They changed it."

"A trap?" Monty asked.

"Don't know," I said. That was the problem with conspiracies. Anything could be everything, but it was just as likely to be nothing. All the more reason to shut this down as soon as we could. "We should be on the lookout just in case. But Conor's right. Getting dunked into a dunk tank isn't really a trap if you're doing it on purpose, and both of them will be doing it. I don't know what she would be trying to accomplish here."

"We can keep posted nearby during the carnival," Conor said. "Make sure no funny business is happening."

I nodded. "Sounds good."

We split up for the day and filled Audrey in once she got back from her appointment.

The next day at school, I spotted Audrey with Sienna in the halls, arms linked as Sienna talked at her, rapid-fire pace.

"Ohmigosh, no way! How are you not already blowing up online? Singers are superhot right now. You should totally collab with me on my next stream!"

I grinned to myself, confident that whatever little

information about her life Sienna didn't immediately post about online, we'd have access to anyway.

Sienna was as protected as we could make her without taking down the BPS, which meant that was next on our list. But it was a pretty big to-do item, and we didn't have a lot of time—not if we wanted to get it done before the dance. It was only a little over a week away.

It wasn't just to protect Sienna, either. Taking out the would-be Snow Princess would be a huge symbolic victory for them, and we couldn't let them have that. That's the kind of thing that makes people escalate. And I knew all about things going too far. I wasn't gonna let that happen at my school.

Not again.

CHAPTER EIGHTEEN
BUG OUT

The trouble started over the weekend.

It was Saturday night, and I was still turning around in my head the best way to take down an entire criminal conspiracy without creating a huge mess when Audrey called.

"Bad news," she said. "The AV kids are negotiating with the anchors. Based on what Steph said, I think the strike will be over by Monday."

I groaned. "Great. All the wrong people are getting along."

"Hey, don't shoot the messenger."

"Sorry. Thanks for telling me. I'm just feeling the pressure here a little bit."

"Hey, don't worry," she said, softening her tone. "You're gonna figure this out. You always do."

"You're not just doing your Face thing to make me feel better, are you?"

"Maybe a little," she admitted, "but only on top of the truth."

I smiled. She always knew what to say. "Hey, while I have you, anything new on the Sienna front?"

"Nope. But I'm sticking to her like glue. She roped me into streaming with her next Wednesday. It's honestly kind of a big honor. She's been in touch with some bakery, and they're gonna send her some products to review. It has a fancy name. Cokesee-something. I think it's French. It's her first sponsored video, so she's super psyched."

"Hmm." If that video blew up it would be more fuel for the fire for Paige. I *really* needed to figure out this plan.

"Hey!" Audrey said sharply. "I can hear your brain grinding. Relax! You got this."

"Thanks, Audrey," I said, but I didn't relax.

On Sunday, like Audrey had predicted, the AV kids reached a truce with the anchors, so on Monday, I met up with Mariposa before school to see if she'd gotten orders to rocket boost Sienna again.

She shook her head as she pocketed a container of maple syrup. "No, and that concerns me. There's no way they didn't know the strike was ending if we knew it was ending, and there's also no way they decided to just let Sienna off the hook so—"

"They must have had a plan B," I finished.

"I would have one," Mariposa said. "And a plan C to be safe."

"And I'm not even done with our plan A," I said.

She smirked. "I bet you wish you believed in rocket boosting people now."

I hated that she was right. Not just about Sienna, about Paige, too. If only it was as easy as taking out one person. Not that I even could since Mariposa couldn't exactly rocket boost her own "boss," but things would be so much easier if I could just make a call and have one person offed. But, lucky me, I had to take down an entire organization.

For the next two days, we kept our eyes open for any sign of a plan B, but nothing emerged. Mariposa didn't get any communications from the BPS. Audrey didn't notice anything strange with Sienna. Monty didn't notice anything off with Paige as he helped with setup for the dance and carnival.

I started keeping an eye on the videos Sienna posted, just to see if I could notice anything strange. It was typical stuff. Daily routine vids. Shopping trips. Vlogs about her day.

I didn't find anything helpful, but it made my stomach feel like an acid pit. She was just a kid in a bad situation that she didn't know she was in. Back at the Grove, I wouldn't have cared if she ended up as collateral damage—it wasn't my problem. But here, I couldn't do that. I knew she didn't deserve whatever the BPS had planned for her.

At lunch on the Wednesday before the dance, Conor thunked his head onto the table dramatically.

"This girl has us running in circles," he said. "This morning I almost put my baby sister on the suspect list for looking at me funny. And I'm only, like, half joking."

"I know," I said. "I'll sleep a lot easier once we put this one to bed. This feels like a puzzle that keeps making new pieces. There's so much to keep track of. All the people and the clubs."

"Hopefully once we have her pinned, *you-know-who* will be scary enough to force the names of all her minions out of her." I doubted anyone in the cafeteria was paying attention to our conversation, but we weren't naming names to play it safe.

And I agreed with Conor. We had a long list of suspects, but we hadn't caught all of them with pencils, so a lot of them were still just strong hunches. And I don't know if it was because it was just me and Conor at the table, like the old days, but a big maybe I hadn't thought about in a while floated into my head.

Malik.

He'd shown up at the start of the month, thrown me into a tailspin, and then disappeared. I'd gotten so caught up with the nitty-gritty of the conspiracy and all our new suspects that he'd gotten lost in the shuffle, but I still didn't trust him.

"What's up?" Conor asked.

"Just thinking."

When he gave me a look that said, *Dude, when are you not?* I added, "About Malik."

"What about him?"

"I don't know. He's a loose end. I don't like loose ends."

"We don't even know if he's connected," he pointed out.

"I know, but it feels too weird to be a coincidence. I just can't think of why they'd bring someone in from the outside. Or how she'd even know him."

Conor pulled out his phone and did some quick swipes. "Hmm, looks like he's friends with Tessa's sister, Regina. And Paige and Tessa are always at each other's houses. If Paige was at Tessa's house at the same time he was there to talk to Regina, that could be a window."

"That gives us a when but not a why." I mentally went through the last jobs we'd done with Malik again. Itsy-Bitsy Spider Job. Alphabet Soup Job. The Busted Ballot Job.

My eyes widened. "Wait! Remember when we rigged that election? Student council rep?"

It was a different kind of race, but an election was an election, and if Paige wanted someone with experience, Malik had it.

Conor dropped his fork and almost jumped out of his seat. "Oh, dude, yeah!" Then he paused. "Wait, but we couldn't crack it, remember? We had to get them to switch to paper ballots we could mess with, because the software was too secure."

"Maybe he figured it out in the meantime," I suggested. "Or maybe he was here to try to figure it out, but it was too hard to crack. Sometimes you get called in for a job and the answer is no can do." I thought back to our encounter and his cocky, gum-chewing swagger. "But then again, two sticks of gum."

"You're really hung up on this gum."

"It's a thing!" I huffed out a breath.

He patted me on the shoulder as he got up. "I'll check out my sites online to see if there have been any cracks to the software since last year when I get home. But, right now, I'm going to the bathroom because my bladder has half a carton of chocolate milk too much in it and I'm about to pop."

I wrinkled my nose. "I don't need a play-by-play, dude."

"Are you sure? It'd make a great article for the school paper."

I threw a Tater Tot at him as he made his way out the door. Then I slid my eyes over to Mariposa. She seemed as calm and collected as ever, but I know I did, too. That didn't mean anything. Jumpy outsides were a luxury we couldn't afford.

But that wasn't the case for everyone in the cafeteria.

I caught motion out of the corner of my eye—the wobble of a nervous walk. I turned to catch a glance at what I assumed was one of Mariposa's unlucky victims for the day and was surprised to see a familiar face.

It was Kennedy.

Kennedy, who I knew didn't have lunch this period.

Kennedy, who I knew didn't have business with Mariposa.

Kennedy, who, as far as I knew, had only one reason to be nervous.

I watched as she walked through the cafeteria, past Mariposa, all the while looking over her shoulder as if she thought she was being watched. She was, of course, but that was all the more reason to act like she wasn't.

This was the reason working with non-pros was so risky. It had taken us forever to train that instinct out of Monty. The BPS operation was big, but it was full of amateurs—which was something I could exploit.

I followed her path as she weaved through tables, stopping in front of a boy I vaguely recognized. He was on our "maybe" list of suspects. Suddenly, I was feeling pretty confident in shifting him to the "confirmed" list.

She opened her shaking hand and showed him something. Then he slipped her a piece of paper. She balled it up in her hand and made for the exit.

I flicked my eyes between Kennedy and the teacher who was giving out hall passes. He had a line of six kids waiting. If I got in line and did this the right way, she could get away. I sat there frozen with indecision for a second before I steeled myself and got up. I didn't have a plan. This wasn't my specialty. But Conor wasn't here, and I couldn't let this opportunity slip.

I shot off a quick text to Conor—*Trailing Kennedy. Think she's up to something.*—before putting my phone on silent and shoving it in my pocket. There's nothing worse than a phone buzzing when you're trying to be stealthy.

Unlike Kennedy, I did my best casual walk, like I didn't care who saw me get up. I was just a kid in a school. What was suspicious about that? I moseyed on over to the bulletin board, all nonchalant, and pretended to study the flyers. Oh, Boy Scout meeting tonight? Cool. Nice and normal, keeping an eye on her the entire time.

As soon as she exited the cafeteria, I picked up speed.

Too fast! A teacher stood in my path.

"Whoa. What's the hurry? You know there's no running in the—"

"My bladder has half a carton of chocolate milk too much in it, and I'm about to pop!"

She couldn't move out of my way fast enough. I guess sometimes you *do* need the play-by-play. Thank you, Conor.

I slipped past her and out the door, just catching Kennedy as she turned a corner. I speed walked through the halls, slowing down at doors with windows and keeping an eye out for any Space Cadets.

A teacher passed. I ducked down and slurped some water from a nearby fountain.

Kennedy turned, and I pretended to be fiddling with a combination lock on one of the lockers—she didn't know which one was mine.

I recognized the path she was taking. She was heading to her locker. Somewhere she felt safe.

I trailed silently behind her, just out of her line of sight, as she keyed in her locker combo and opened the door, so she could read the note behind the false privacy it provided.

She looked over her shoulder one more time, and I walked past her, doubling back with lightning speed the moment she turned back to the note.

She was blocking my view, so I couldn't see, but she wasn't that tall. I stood on my tiptoes, trying to catch a glimpse of something, anything, one word, one letter, one—

"Let me see some hall passes!" a voice barked.

Kennedy yelped, swiftly turning and clutching the slip of paper in her hand but too slow. The new arrival snatched it away from her, glancing at it before handing it back.

"That's not a hall pass! Show me a real one or—"

"I have one!" she said hurriedly, fishing a piece of paper from her pocket and handing it over.

The cadet adjusted his badge and squinted at the hall pass before shoving it back at her.

"All right, but you better get to wherever you're supposed to be or I'm writing you up! And that'll be on your permanent record!"

The threat of a smudge on her perfect record sent her scurrying—I don't think she even registered that I was there. As she turned the corner, the cadet turned to me.

"And where's *your* hall pass?"

I slapped him on the shoulder.

"Knock it off, Conor. And thanks for the save."

He winked at me. "No prob. Leave the trailing to the experts next time."

"I will when you stop taking inconvenient bathroom breaks. Maybe lay off the chocolate milk while we're in go mode. And where did you get the badge?"

He grinned. "I told you I was working with Monty on forgeries. Looks good, right? Shout out to his brother for working at an art-supply store. I've been waiting for a chance to test this, and when I got your text, I figured it was a good time to bust it out."

"Good thing you did because I did *not* have a plan to get that note. Speaking of, what did it say?"

"It said 'Ladybug is on.' But I have no idea what that means."

"I think it must be whatever their plan B is. But I don't know what it could be."

It had to be some kind of code name, but without more information, it didn't tell us anything. Still, it was a start at least.

"Let's get this to Mariposa. She might be able to find out more."

I passed off the info to Mariposa before lunch finished, and she promised to see what she could dig up. I also told Audrey to keep an extra close eye on Sienna, which she said was no problem.

"I'm hanging with her at her place after school to stream, remember?"

The rest of us went to Conor's place once school was over. Conor still felt pretty sure that Malik wouldn't have been able to crack the voting software, but we wanted to be certain. Voting closed tomorrow, Thursday, after the carnival, so if it was being rigged, we needed to know ASAP.

Monty couldn't help with the techy stuff, so he was in the kitchen making cookies when we got a text from Audrey.

I read it and frowned. "She says Sienna is doing her live stream at school. That she got special permission to use their setup to film."

"So?" asked Conor. "AV Club has good stuff. Like

lighting and tripods and stuff. She's into production value, so it's right up her alley."

I shook my head. "This doesn't feel right. She's alone at school the same day we learn some kind of mysterious plan is a go? I don't trust that."

Conor checked his phone. "She's not streaming yet. We have, like, twenty-five minutes."

I shot off a text to Audrey: *Why at school? Is that new?*

A ping came back a minute later: *New student government initiative. Making club resources more readily available school-wide. Are we suspicious?*

Me: *We're highly suspicious.*

Audrey: *Let me know if you need her stalled.*

Monty walked in, dusting his hands off on his pants. "Cookies are in the oven!" he said happily. "Should be about ten minutes." He paused. "Is something happening?"

"We think Sienna might be about to get got," Conor said.

"Isn't she with Audrey?" Monty asked.

"Yeah, but they're at school, which is super suspicious," said Conor.

"They're live streaming an unboxing of some product,"

I said. "Audrey said it was some French bakery thing. Cokesee-something."

Monty's face went still. "Was it Coccinelle?" He pronounced it *Coke-see-nelle*.

"Could be? Audrey wasn't sure. Why?"

"*Coccinelle* is French for 'ladybug.'"

CHAPTER NINETEEN
SPECIAL DELIVERY

I had Audrey on the phone in no seconds flat.

"Audrey, it's a trap!"

"What are you talking about?"

"The unboxing. It's the BPS. I don't know how, but that French word you said? Monty translated it. It means 'ladybug.'"

Conor motioned me over to his laptop frantically.

"Hold on, Conor has something. I'll put you on speaker."

"Look at this!" Conor said. "You can buy three thousand live ladybugs online for less than ten bucks. How much you wanna bet there's a nasty surprise in that box?"

I couldn't help but flash back to the Itsy-Bitsy Spider Job and the panic one bug had produced. Even if she didn't have a full-on phobia like my old target Mr. Danvers did, three thousand was *way* more than one. Anyone would freak. If Conor's hunch was correct, she would not like that one bit. Not only that, she'd be releasing three thousand live ladybugs on school property. I didn't know if that disqualified you from the running for Snow Princess, but I couldn't imagine it would help.

"OK, yikes," Audrey said. "I know she hates bugs. She flips out like a cartoon character. But are you sure? She's been emailing with these people for a few days. I've seen the box. It looks legit."

"So does the paperwork that Mariposa made for the school paper," I said. "That doesn't mean anything. A few days would fit the timeline. It was tight, but the BPS would have enough time. But there's no way to be one hundred percent sure without checking the box. Can you take a peek?"

"No," she said. "It's tied all fancy. I couldn't retie it without her noticing. And if it is ladybugs, they'll just get out once I open it."

"Hmm, good point," Conor said. "You'll have to smash the box, then."

"*What?*" she yelped, voice pitching. "I can't do that!"

"Why not?"

"Because either it's fancy baked goods, in which case, I'm ruining her unboxing, or it's ladybugs, in which case I'm killing innocent ladybugs!"

Conor looked at me and Monty in disbelief and then yelled into the phone, "*They're bugs!*"

"*Innocent bugs!*" she yelled back. "Monty, back me up here."

"She's right, Conor," Monty said, crossing his arms. "That's mean."

Conor raked a hand through his hair with frustration. "I can't believe y'all are making me miss Mariposa."

"OK, OK, OK," I said, taking a breath. We didn't have time to argue. We needed another plan.

"Can you just steal the box from her?" I asked. "Catch and release?"

"If I had backup, maybe," she said. "But she's not letting it out of her sight. And if she opens it and it's an empty box, that's also going to be a problem."

"Should we just tell her what's going on?" Monty suggested. "Then we wouldn't have to steal it."

Conor snorted. "This girl vlogs every second of her

life she's allowed to have a phone. Do you think she can keep a secret?"

"We're running out of time," Audrey said sharply. "What do you want me to do? And don't say smash the box because— *Oh, Sienna!* No, I'm fine, just talking to my mom really quick. Yeah, one second and I'll help you with setting up. I just need to find out if I should *shovel the snow myself or if I should ask for help.*"

"I'm still team Hulk smash," Conor said.

"Maybe she can keep a secret if it's important," Monty said.

"Mom?" Audrey said.

The boys looked at me expectantly. It was my call. I looked at Conor. I looked at Monty. I smelled the scent of half-baked cookies floating in from the kitchen.

"Audrey, stall her as long as you can. And send me a picture of the box. I have a plan. I'll text you." I hung up the phone and turned to the guys. "OK, I think we can do this, but we have to work fast." My phone pinged as a picture of the box came in. It was wrapped up like a Christmas present with fancy gold wrapping paper and an elaborate red bow. I showed it to Monty.

"You're the arts-and-crafts whiz. Can you tie a bow like this?"

"I think so."

"Good. And we need to get to school pronto."

"It'll take longer than twenty minutes to walk," Conor said. "Probably longer than Audrey can stall."

"I'm not planning on walking," I said, heading for the door. "Your sister is home, and she has a car."

He snorted. "Good luck getting her to give you a ride."

"I don't need luck," I said, heading for Bethany's room. "I have my share of the heist profits."

Bethany actually wasn't in her room. She was in the living room, fully zombied out watching some anime and eating chips directly out of the bag while her textbooks lay on the ground in front of her, abandoned.

Before I opened my mouth she said, "DJ, this better be good," without even turning to see who it was. "I do not want to leave this couch unless someone is on fire. And, like, someone I care about, not some rando."

I decided the direct approach was best. I slammed a wad of Starcade receipts on the table in front of her. "This is enough for a Bluetooth speaker from the

Starcade. You can flip it online for about sixty bucks. That's enough for a weekend pass for the summer anime con. I need a ride."

She looked over at the receipts, then at me.

"I'll get my keys."

Fifteen minutes later, Beth had dropped us off and I was running at full tilt to the AV room. I pounded on the door when I reached it, disheveled and out of breath.

Sienna opened the door, looking halfway between confused and annoyed. The box was sitting near her on a table that had a tripod placed in front of it with her phone mounted on it.

"DJ? What are you doing here? This isn't a good time. I'm already late. Consistency is very important for growing an audience, you know."

"I'm sorry, just, is Audrey here? I need to talk to her. Alone."

Audrey slid into view on a swivel chair.

"Is something wrong?" Sienna asked.

"No! I mean not really, I mean . . ." I swallowed, cupped my hands around Sienna's left ear, and whispered, "I'm going to ask Audrey to the dance, but I can't do it in front of you. Can you leave for a second?"

To say she lit up would be an understatement. You could have set up a dozen more ring lights in the room and it wouldn't have made her look any brighter. She couldn't have gotten out of the room fast enough. She punched me in the shoulder as she left.

"Get 'em, Romeo."

When I turned, Audrey was already unwrapping the box as quickly as she could without ripping the paper. I vaulted across the room to open a window.

"Romeo?" she asked. "What did you say to her?"

"Later," I answered, throwing open the window.

Conor and Monty were waiting outside.

"All right," she said, "but I'm holding you to that."

"Did you get it?" Conor asked.

In response, she handed over the unwrapped box and closed the window. Once it was fully sealed, I flashed a thumbs-up and Conor opened the box.

There was a moment of stillness before thousands of ladybugs began to swarm—some crawling, some flying, all very alive and eager to leave. Conor tipped the box over, tapping the bottom to get them out quicker.

"Don't hurt them!" Monty squeaked, and Conor tapped the box the tiniest bit more gently.

As I watched the ladybugs fly away, I felt a pang of relief. At first, I thought it was just because we'd been right and gotten here in time, but it felt bigger than that. Bigger than these bugs. Bigger than Sienna. Bigger than this job, even.

I thought about the conversation I'd run away from with David.

"Have you ever considered that maybe, sometimes, the reason you won't take a break is that you're overcompensating for—"

He was right.

No matter how many jobs I did, the Itsy-Bitsy Spider Job stuck with me, like the stink from gym shorts you couldn't quite get clean. Even though I knew my new crew didn't judge me and I was trying to do better now, the fact that I'd gotten away with it felt slimy.

But watching the ladybugs scurry away somehow made my guilt feel a little lighter.

I took a deep breath.

I'm sorry, Mr. Danvers.

I'm sorry, anyone else I hurt.

I'm doing better now.

I promise.

I blew out the breath, and Audrey tilted her head at me.

"Are you good?" she asked.

I smiled. "I'm great."

Once all the ladybugs were gone, Monty tossed in his cookies wrapped in parchment paper and started rewrapping the box with lightning speed. Either his origami lesson had paid off or he was a natural. It was done in a snap, and I reopened the window to grab it.

"Great work, guys. I'll meet you by the car in a minute."

They nodded and hightailed it away while I put the box back where it had been.

"We'll stay close in case the BPS tries any other shenanigans," I said. "Text us if you need us. Or signal—we'll watch the live stream. Oh, and we need to fill in Mariposa."

"I'll be fine," she said, pushing me toward the door. "Just go before Sienna gets suspicious."

"Yeah, I'm out. Oh, wait."

She stopped pushing. "What?"

"One last thing before I go. Can you scream *Yes!* like you're excited?"

"Why?"

"I told Sienna I was asking you to the dance."

"*What?*"

"I know, I know. But I couldn't think of anything else she'd leave for, so can you just—"

"Yes!" Audrey squealed, summoning Sienna back into the room like a homing pigeon. Her eyes sparkled with nosy curiosity.

"What happened? What did I miss? Give me the scoop!"

I pushed past her and out the door. "Seeyoulater Audreybye!" My words rushed out all in one breath; I was only halfway acting. I was very happy in that moment that I wasn't the Face of the group.

The live stream went off without a hitch. Sienna raved about the slightly underdone but still delicious cookies provided to her by the Coccinelle bakery.

"They almost taste right out of the oven," she said.

If she only knew.

While Audrey was finishing up with Sienna, we video called Mariposa from the parking lot to fill her in on the new situation.

"After school," she said, eyes widening slightly. "They planned this for after school? That's . . . concerning."

"Yeah, I was thinking the same thing," I said. School was one thing, but after school? Not even during a club? Were there any limits to what they'd do? Would they have tried this same trick at her house? Was anywhere safe? "We're lucky we caught this in time."

"Yeah," Conor chimed in. "Monty is MVP for sure. If he didn't know what that word meant, it would be ladybug city in there right now."

He blushed. "Aww, it's no big deal."

"No, seriously, dude," Conor insisted. "Since when do you know French?"

"His last name is LaCroix," Mariposa deadpanned, leaving the *you idiot* at the end implied.

"I also know some Arabic, from my mom's side!" he added cheerily.

"Dude, *what*? How has this never come up before?"

He shrugged. "You never asked."

Before Conor could start grilling Monty about his family tree, on the off chance of shaking loose anything else interesting, Audrey jogged up.

"Oof," she said, resting her forehead against Monty's shoulder. "I can't believe that worked. I need to lie down."

"Hey, Audrey," Conor said. "Did you know Monty speaks Arabic?"

"Uh, yeah," she said, voice muffled by Monty's shirt. "Haven't you met his mom?"

"As fascinating as this discussion is," Mariposa cut in, "we don't have time for this. Not if you all insist on keeping this girl safe. This was a clear escalation. Do you think they're going to stop here?"

"She's right," I said. "They were watching this broadcast just like us. They know their plan B for *bug* was stopped. They're probably already putting some kind of plan C in motion."

"So, what do we do?" Monty asked. "How do we take them down for good?"

I sighed. That was the million-dollar question.

This wasn't just one person we had to deal with. This was an entire tangle of people to take down. A twisted mess. I'd wanted to deal with this delicately. There was no telling what kind of ripple effects just taking out the queenpin would have. But it didn't seem like we had a choice.

"Guys, they're forcing our hand here. I think we have to go for the nuclear option. Take out Paige directly. Expose this to the principal. And we do it tomorrow. At the carnival."

"Tomorrow?" Audrey said. "That's such short notice."

"I know," I said, "but that's why we have to do it. They won't expect something on such a quick turnaround. And Paige will be dealing with the carnival, the dance, and being a nominee on top of the BPS stuff. It's the most off guard we'll ever be able to catch her."

"I agree that we need to strike now," Mariposa said. "But involving the school admin? Are you sure? We don't make it a habit to tangle with them for obvious reasons."

"You use the school system to rocket boost people," Monty pointed out.

"Yeah, but that doesn't involve actual teachers. We prefer to handle things in-house."

"We do, too, but I don't see another option here," I said. "They're trading in symbols, so we should, too. We can't let them get away with more than they already have. If they can make Paige Snow Princess, we're in a lot of trouble. We'll have a lot of cleanup work to do afterward, but we can worry about that later."

"Do you already have something in mind?" Audrey asked.

"Yeah," I said. "Modification of what we planned when we sent you after Mariposa, except we'll sub her in for you. I don't think Paige is doing a lot of talking directly to her minions, but she might make an exception for Mariposa since she's such a big fish. If we can get Paige to admit it while we're recording and send that to the principal, we'll be set."

"Mm-hm, and you're one hundred percent certain Conor will make sure I don't *also* get caught?" Mariposa asked.

"Two hundred percent," Conor said confidently. "Once I have the recording, I can pitch your voice up or down or cut it out entirely."

"And I'll give you an alibi if you need it," said Audrey. "Plus, most people won't be brave enough to say anything against you."

"Right," I agreed. "The BPS is on the come up, but you've been established for longer, and you're pretty scary. No offense."

"That's the whole point, so none taken." She pursed

her lips together in thought. "Lucky comes back on Friday. He's milked his injury for as long as he can. And I hate to say it, but I don't have a cleaner plan. I'll go with you on this. But if anything goes wrong—"

"It won't," I said. "We'll prep all of tonight. This will go off without a hitch. We work on a shorter timetable than this all the time."

I hoped I sounded confident. I felt confident, but that was only because I wouldn't let myself feel anything else. There would be time for that after this was over. I hadn't wanted to take a break before this all started, but now I would give anything for a nice, normal, boring day with my friends.

We arranged for an in-person meetup the next day after school to go over details, and then Beth chauffeured us all back home.

We dropped Audrey home first since she lived the closest, and, right as she left, I stopped her.

"Wait."

"What's wrong?" she asked.

"What did you tell Sienna?" I asked. "You know about the . . ." I could sense Conor's ears pricking at the conversation, so I trailed off. "You know."

"Oh," she said. "Don't worry about that."

I frowned. "What does that mean?"

She gave me a smile that was halfway to a smirk. "It means what it means. If you have something to say to me after this is all done, then all right, but right now? Head in the game, Darius James."

I shivered.

"'Darius James.' Am I in trouble?"

"We're all in trouble," she said with a wink before waving and running off to her front door.

Bethany had been mostly ignoring us, as usual, but she watched Audrey leave with a raised eyebrow and then turned to look at me.

"It sounds like you have some problems to solve, little man."

I slammed the door closed.

"You don't know the half of it."

CHAPTER TWENTY
FUN AND GAMES

There's nothing like an excuse to get out of class. Field trip, pep rally, fire drill—even the nerdiest kid appreciates the break. And there's no break like a carnival.

My reporter credentials were enough to get me out of class early. Honestly, I felt stupid for not inventing a fake newspaper earlier; it opened a lot of doors.

It was near the end of sixth period, and the carnival started officially in seventh. Tessa was going to show us around, let us try the food, and take some pics before her carefully organized event was swarmed with restless students let off their leashes.

I met Audrey in the hall on the way to the gym. As soon as she saw me, she jumped right into status updates.

"Conor's out on a hall pass. He's getting Mariposa all rigged up for audio. I checked on them on the way here.

They'll give us the all clear once they're ready, but wait to send her in until they get the signal from us. Conor will be waiting in the bathroom."

"Great, and Monty should already be inside." Space Cadets were helping with last-minute setup, which meant he could also monitor the situation and let us know if anything fishy was going on.

We were hoping to get everything we needed before the actual carnival started. Tessa and Paige were running the thing, so they'd be overseeing. Audrey would lure Paige away from Tessa and toward Mariposa, who would ask to talk to Paige in private. And I was confident Mariposa could hold her own. It was Mariposa. This part of the plan should be a slam dunk. So why did I feel uneasy?

"Nervous?" said Audrey.

"No, I just . . . I don't know, I feel weird. Like I'm missing something." I tried to smother it with a smile. "I know, I know. Stop connecting dots after we already connected them."

"No," she said. "I trust you. Don't do that DJ thing and keep it locked in your head. If you think something's wrong, tell me. Tell us. We'll help. I know you're the Brains, but the rest of us are pretty good, too, you know."

I smiled. "I'll keep that in mind. Now, are you ready?"

She flashed a double thumbs-up. "Let's do this. If we're fast, we can even enjoy the carnival after . . . as reporters, of course."

The idea of just doing stuff with Audrey at school in public in general was new, but the thought of going to the carnival with her made my stomach feel extra fluttery. I never wanted to finish a job faster in my life.

When we swung open the doors to the gym, we saw that Tessa had made good on her promise to make this the best carnival possible. The setup was amazing. Banners, prize booths, games, popcorn, churros, cotton candy, doughnuts in the school colors, and kid-friendly versions of definitely-not-kid-friendly music playing in the background. One corner of the room was dominated by two big booths—a pieing station and a dunk tank.

It seemed like everything Tessa had promised was there—except for Tessa herself. And I also didn't see Paige. I looked over at Audrey, who said, "Yeah, I don't see them, either."

I checked my watch and then scanned the room again. They were nowhere to be seen. I did however see Monty, hauling a pallet of chips toward the food table. We flagged him down.

"Monty!" I hissed. "Where are they? Paige and Tessa? Are they together?"

"I dunno," he said. "Neither of them were here when I got here. Caro is in charge. I would have texted but—"

"LaCroix!" Caro barked from the other side of the room. "We have less than five minutes before this thing starts. Why are you chatting?"

"Sorry, Caro!" he called before blurting out, "Nothing seems fishy so far, but I'll let you know," and going back to get another pallet of chips.

There was a ping on my phone. I made sure I wasn't in view of any teachers, or worse, Caro, before I checked it. It was from Conor. *Good 2 Go. Should I send in 🦋?*

Not yet, I texted back. *Paige and Tessa missing.*

"Maybe we should ask someone," Audrey suggested. "Like . . . oh! Santiago?"

Santiago was standing near the dunk tank, testing the chair mechanism. He pounded his fist on the target, and the empty seat flipped down over a pool of red water.

"I hope it's supposed to be that color," Audrey joked, pointing it out.

"What? Oh, yeah. Food coloring. You know, for our school colors? Go Rockets and all that. Don't worry, it'll just wash out with water. We tested it. Did you need something?"

"Yeah," said Audrey. "Do you know where Paige and Tessa are?"

"Umm, not sure," said Santiago. "Tessa said Paige had some kind of surprise? I don't know what that means, though."

Audrey and I looked at each other. Paige and Tessa were missing and together. This felt fishy.

"Oh, I just remembered a newspaper thing we have to do—later, Santiago," I said, steering Audrey away.

Audrey could have gotten us out of there more smoothly, but I didn't want to wait.

"I don't like this," I said.

"Do you think Tessa's in danger?" Audrey asked.

"I don't think so, but we need to be sure. Can you sneak out and do a quick scan for them? I want Conor to stay with Mariposa and his tech."

She nodded before heading off. "Text me if you need me."

"I will."

I texted the group about the change, then I started to circulate, taking pictures, scanning the room, checking the door every time it opened. Soon the bell rang, and kids started pouring into the gym. I spotted Tyler, who waved at me.

"Yo, Deej!" he said, stopping when he saw the camera. "Oh, my bad. Reporter Deej. Very nice."

"Haha, yeah," I said, trying to figure out the fastest way to exit this conversation that I knew most people in this gym would kill for. "Hey, don't you have to get to your booth?"

"Yeah, man, I'm on my way there. Do you need a picture of me for the paper? You know, since I'm a nominee and all?"

"Yeah," I said, "but don't worry. I'll take some once you're pied. That will be more fun."

"Gotcha, gotcha." He clapped me on the back, then leaned in close. "Protip, though, make sure you get a pic of Sienna *before* she gets dunked. If you take a picture of her when she looks like a drowned rat, she's gonna go ballistic on you."

"Good to know," I said as if I already didn't.

"All right, see you later, man."

I was about to grab my phone to check in with Audrey when someone from behind me called, "Hey, DJ!"

It was Tessa, sauntering up casually, hands in her pockets. "Santiago said you were looking for me."

"Yeah," I said, flicking my eyes past her as subtly as I could to check for Paige. They were always together. Where was Paige? "You said you were going to meet us, remember?"

"I know, I know, I'm sorry," she said, pulling her hands out of her pockets so she could gesture. "There was this whole thing I had to take care of and—"

"Whoa!" I said as I saw her palms. They were blood red. "You're not—"

She looked confused, then her eyes went wide. "Nonononono! Don't worry! It's not blood. Geez, can you imagine? No, it's wool dye. You know, like, for sheep? It stains really badly. Trust me, I speak from experience."

"Wool dye?" Why would there be wool dye at a carnival?

What would you do with it? Where would you even get it?

"Yeah," she answered. "Paige spilled it on me by accident."

A farm! You'd get wool dye at a farm, like the one Paige lived on. And you could use it to—

"DJ!" It was Monty, rushing up to me.

"Wha—" I started, but he just took my shoulders and pointed me to the corner of the room.

"Paige is here."

There she was, in a big shirt and shorts, right next to Sienna, who was climbing the stairs and sitting on her little seat above the water. The water that was dyed red. And Paige's hands? Also red.

Oh no.

If Sienna went into the stained water, she'd get red dye all over her. Her fair skin would probably be stained for days. And the dance was this Saturday. If she skipped picture day over a "challenging hair day," she definitely wouldn't show up to the dance looking like a lobster.

If Paige couldn't get Sienna suspended and she couldn't rig the vote, she could knock out her competition. Plans A, B, and C.

My brain was doing the 100 meter, but everything around me felt like it was in slow motion. Tyler was standing behind the line, holding a baseball while Sienna batted her eyelashes and said something at him. His lips curled into a smile, and he wound up.

I locked eyes with Monty.

"Stop that ball."

Without another question, Monty bolted, moving a lot faster and more gracefully than it seemed like he should be able to.

Tessa's eyes bugged out. "What— Oh my gosh! What are you—?"

I ignored her as I watched the ball fly out of Tyler's hand at the top of his always perfect arc, sail forward, and—

WHAM!

I hissed in sympathy pain as it smacked right into Monty's chest. He didn't flinch, but I knew it had to hurt. I made a mental note to spend a lot of tickets on something nice for him when the job was done.

Tessa still looked shocked. "DJ! Why did you do that?"

"I'll explain later. Trust me!" I rushed toward the dunk tank, doing my best to be subtle, which wasn't too hard because everyone who'd been watching was mainly trying to figure out what the heck had just happened.

Monty flicked his eyes over at me like *Help!*, so I elbowed a stack of plastic cups on a table as I passed. Not everyone turned at the clattering sounds they made as they hit the ground, but it was enough for Monty to slip away from the center of attention.

It was fine, I thought as I kept moving. It was just going to add to his mysterious aura. *Did you hear that big kid made Tyler throw a baseball at him at one hundred miles an hour for fun?* People believed weirder stuff about him.

As I reached the tank, Sienna preened. "Oh, there you are. If you want to take a picture, then—"

I ignored her and stuck my hand into the tank. My skin was darker than Sienna's, but so was Tessa's, and her palms were stained, which means that when I took my hand out, then I should—

Tessa grabbed me by the shoulder and pulled me away from the tank.

"DJ!" she said, steering me to the other side of the room. "You should definitely take some pictures of the *whattheheck-areyoudoing?*" she hissed once we were away from the crowd.

"Listen, I know it sounds crazy, but—" I raised my hand so she'd see me red-handed, literally red-handed—but there was no staining like on Tessa's hands. The color was diluted. More pink than red, and it ran right off.

"But?" Tessa prompted.

"I—"

"There you are, DJ!" Audrey said, grabbing my shoulder just like Tessa had, but this time, it felt like a relief. I'd never been so happy to be manhandled in my life. "Tessa, one sec," she said, dragging me away before Tessa had a chance to object.

"What was that?" Audrey asked. "I saw her drag you away from the dunk tank."

"Dye on Tessa's hands," I said. "Wool dye. Like on a farm. And dye in the tank. And I saw it on Paige, too, and I thought—"

Audrey shook her head subtly and pulled out her phone. "I found Tessa and Paige, but I got caught by the principal. He wanted to walk me to the gym, and I couldn't text while we were talking. But I was about to send you this."

She showed me a picture of Paige with the principal. She was helping him dye his hair bright red.

"It's the surprise for hitting the food drive target," she said. "I don't think it has anything to do with the BPS."

I felt like I was the one who'd gotten a baseball beamed at my chest. Bad call. I'd made a bad call. And now Tessa was suspicious and Monty was gonna have a bruise and Paige—

"DJ," Audrey said, snapping me out of my head. "What's happening? What do you want us to do?"

Right. The job was still on. Mariposa was still with Conor, prepped to record and ready for a signal. I could beat myself up later. I had to make sure this hiccup didn't completely derail this train.

"Uh, OK. The plan is the same. Text Conor and Mariposa. Get Paige to them. She's getting ready to get dunked, so it might be a little trickier, but—"

"Don't worry," she said. "I got this. And you?"

"I need to smooth things over with Tessa so the 'school newspaper' doesn't get shut down," I said with air quotes. "And I wanna keep her busy so she's not wondering where Paige is."

She nodded. "Got it. I'll ping you when we're done."

I watched her walk over to the dunk tank, talk to a very confused-looking Paige, and then link arms with her as she headed for the door. It was a really familiar thing to do, but Audrey had a way of putting people at ease.

Which left me with Tessa. By the time I turned back to her, she was talking to Santiago. I hoped the busyness meant she had too much going on to remember to call me out—at least until we'd caught Paige in our trap.

I thought about just slipping away while she was distracted, but I needed to keep eyes on her and make sure she didn't cross paths with Paige or the team. It was important to keep track of all the pieces on the board.

"I think we're gonna run out of cups," Santiago was saying when I walked up.

"Are there no more in the back?" she asked. "I thought we planned for this."

"A bunch just got knocked over by accident, and I think people are throwing them out, not reusing them like we thought they would."

She sighed.

"Hey," I said, feeling slightly guilty. "Do you guys need cups? We got a lot more than we needed for the wrap party for the musical last year. We could go to the auditorium and get them. I think they're backstage."

Whatever confusion and annoyance she'd been feeling toward me before seemed to be water *waaay* under the bridge. Nothing to smooth over your image in someone's eyes like being the person with the solution.

"You're a lifesaver. Thanks, DJ. Come on. Let's hurry before they run out."

As the three of us walked out the door, we passed Principal Bowman, who was standing right outside the door like Audrey had said, wearing a hat to hide his freshly dyed red hair.

"Regina!" he said, before tapping his forehead apologetically. "Sorry. Tessa. You just—"

"Look so much alike," Tessa said with the rhythm of a thing you've said a million times before. Something flashed across her face, too quickly for me to read, and it was replaced by an easy smile. "Can't wait for your big entrance. I'll be right back to announce it."

"Looking forward to it," he said. "This was a great idea. And I think the dance might even be as good as last year's."

Another flash, just as unreadable. But . . . it felt familiar. When had I seen this before?

"Thanks, Principal Bowman. Be back in a sec."

We made our way down the hall toward the auditorium, and I racked my brain. I wasn't sure what I'd seen, but it wasn't happy. She'd bounced back to happy, but there'd been something before that. And why did it seem familiar? When had I ever seen Tessa even a little bit upset—minus the dunk tank incident from five minutes ago?

We stepped into the auditorium, Santiago holding the door open for us.

"Where are the cups?" Tessa asked.

"In the back," I said, pointing. "In the prop closet, I think." I walked down the aisle in the middle of the room and ran back in my head the conversations I'd had with Tessa. She hadn't liked it when it seemed like we were accusing Paige, but that didn't seem relevant. And she didn't like anything that might mess with the carnival or the dance, but that wasn't it. In fact, Principal Bowman had said the dance might have been as good as the year before, when she ran it with her sister.

Her sister. She'd reacted at her sister's name way back when we'd interviewed her. Audrey asked her if she was the reason she ran for president and she'd rolled her eyes.

People had beef all the time, and I noticed but I didn't

go around prying—it wasn't any of my business. But . . . something about this felt off. I had a feeling. And Audrey had just told me to trust my feelings. There was something with her sister. I had to chase that.

"So," I said as I neared the stage. "Has winter formal planning been easier or harder for you?" I asked.

"Easier or harder than what?" Tessa asked.

"Last year," I said. "You know, since you don't have your sister around?"

There was the face twitch again! I had a better read on it now that I'd been expecting it. It was like I'd personally insulted her. Like I'd slapped her in the face. All in a microsecond.

"I haven't really thought about it," she said.

Lie. That was a lie. You didn't react like that about things you didn't think about.

I started up the stairs, making sure to look over my shoulder so I could read her as she followed behind me. "I bet it's pros and cons. On the one hand, no more help. On the other hand, my best friend has an older sister, and I bet he'd be so annoyed if they went to the same school. You're probably happy she's in high school now."

She made a noncommittal humming sound.

I kept pushing. "I mean, she's not around to bug you. Or snitch on you. My friend says his sister snitches on him a lot. And with her gone that means you get to be . . . president."

I felt my blood turn to slushy, cold and thick and slow in my veins.

Number two. This whole conspiracy had to do with being number two. Second chair. Second string. Second best. Paige was vice president. She was number two to Tessa's number one. But Tessa also was number two. Not to anyone in the school. To her *sister*. To Regina. Anything Paige would have had access to, so would Tessa. And we hadn't been watching her closely, except as a possible target. Why would we think she'd be anything but a target? She was second to nobody—no one here anyway.

It was Tessa. The whole time it had been Tessa, and I was here alone with her, having this realization while looking her dead in the eyes.

"DJ?" she said, tilting her head slightly.

Jumpy insides, cool outsides. Jumpy insides, cool outsides. Jumpy insides, cool outsides.

"Yeah, yeah, sorry. I just remembered, the cups actually aren't in the prop closet. They're in the choir room. That's my bad. I can just run over and get them."

"Oh, you're doing us a favor already, don't go alone. Santiago and I will go with you."

"No!" I yelled, a tiny bit too forcefully. I smoothed out my voice to be casual, chill, and not as jumpy as my insides currently were. "Don't worry, you don't have to come with me. I'll do it."

"I'm in charge of the carnival," she said easily. "It wouldn't be fair for me to make you do my dirty work." She smiled. "And it will be faster if we all help."

I wasn't Audrey. I couldn't charm my way out of the room. But maybe I didn't need to leave the room.

"Oh, you know what, I can just have someone get it for us. Gimme a sec." I pulled out my phone.

She frowned slightly. "DJ, there's no texting during class hours."

"It's fine. We're not in class," I said, flipping over to the group text and tapping out a message. "Don't worry, it'll only take a—"

I suddenly felt the phone being snatched out of my

hand. I turned. Santiago. I widened my eyes. Space Cadets weren't allowed to confiscate phones.

"I'm gonna have to insist," she said, her tone suddenly laced with steel. When I turned back to her, I saw a look I'd seen in Lucky's eyes before. In Mariposa's eyes. In my eyes.

"We don't want you texting any of your friends before we have a chance to talk." She nodded at Santiago, who crossed his arms and planted his feet, as if daring me to run.

I was made. Playing dumb wouldn't help. Maybe an appeal to his sense of honor? "You're a Space Cadet!" I said. "You can't do this! You're like one of the top guys!"

"I'm *vice* captain," he said, crossing his arms. "For now."

Tessa reached out her hand, and Santiago gave her my phone. She scrolled through the open messages for a few seconds, then looked back at me.

"All right, DJ. Let's talk."

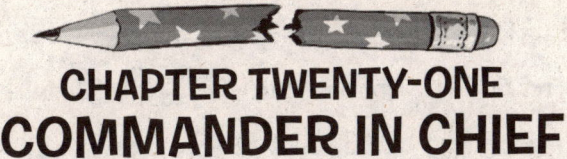

CHAPTER TWENTY-ONE
COMMANDER IN CHIEF

We'd been wrong.

Not about everything. There was a conspiracy, and it was made up of all the number two people in the school, but the person at the center wasn't Paige. It was Tessa. Beloved Tessa. Popular Tessa. President Tessa.

She hadn't said it yet, but she didn't have to. The way she was looking at me was enough—not to mention her having Santiago snatch my phone and block me from leaving. I glanced over at him. He'd been the one to bust Choi. Monty had made it sound like a coincidence. Now it was looking more like a setup.

I quickly ran through options in my head. I could run, but I wouldn't get too far without Santiago grabbing me. Clearly, he was willing to get physical enough to snatch things from me. Would he take it further? On the other hand, I didn't even know what Tessa wanted.

She couldn't keep me here forever. Maybe I could let her talk until I could figure something out. Or until the rest of the team came to find me! They'd finish with Paige soon enough and wonder where I was. I just had to hold on until then.

Plan in place, I turned my full attention to Tessa.

"So, BPS. That's you. The whole time it's been you." I didn't phrase it like a question, and I didn't lead up to it. There was no point. We both knew what was going on.

"Not just me," she said. "I know you've been playing detective. It was my vision, but it's not just me. Athletes, artists, kids from the entire school are working together to make things more fair."

"Fair? Tessa, you sabotaged the spelling bee. You rigged an art competition. You were gonna cause a ladybug-pocalypse! How is that fair?"

She raised an eyebrow. "You break into lockers. You get exams canceled. How is *that* fair?"

I thought I'd made my peace with what we did, but I still felt a twinge of defensiveness. "That's different."

"Is it?"

"Yes! We're helping people."

"Hmm. You weren't here last year, but you're a smart kid. I'm sure you already know this, but I'm going to tell you anyway. Politics aren't about competence. They're about popularity."

I knew that. I think most regular kids knew that, too. Even if the candidates talked about their platforms and campaigns and all the good they wanted to do, at the end of the day it basically always came down to who was more popular.

"We shouldn't have won," Tessa said. "Regina and me. Harry was a better speaker; he had a better platform; he was a nicer person. But Regina was more popular, so she got what she wanted. Just like always."

"Maybe she was just the better candidate."

Her eyes narrowed. "I know she wasn't. Because I know her. And I know how she always gets her way."

"So this is personal."

"Just because I know something personally, doesn't mean it's personal." She took a breath. "And besides, it's not about her. She's not even here anymore." The second part was true, but I didn't believe the first. Whatever else this was about, this absolutely was about Tessa's feelings toward her sister.

"Once Regina was gone, I could finally run on my own," she continued. "Finally do some good. Finally have some control. Do you remember what my current big initiative is?"

"The club surveys," I realized, thinking back to the conversation. She was literally going club to club, gathering information about who was disgruntled enough to join her little operation! It was right in my face, and I'd missed it!

"The first club I shadowed was a new one. The online gaming club. They really had to fight to get that approved. And by 'they' I mean Lane Porter. He spent his entire sixth-grade year working to get that off the ground. He met with the principal. There was a petition. He spearheaded the whole thing. They were having elections when I met with them. You'd think he'd be a shoo-in for president, right?"

"I mean, I kinda doubt you'd be telling me this story otherwise."

She made a *hmm* sound in the back of her throat. "He brought the entire club into existence with a year's worth of work, and they were going to elect Robert Owens student body president because he said his rich dad would buy them all laptops if they did. Blatant bribery! Completely against the rules. But no one cared! Lane didn't even think it was worth trying to report it! No one was going to do anything about it. And do you know what you are if you see something bad happening and let it happen? A part of the problem. They left me in a room alone with the ballots for a few minutes. So . . . I lost some. The right person won."

My ears pricked at that. The election. She'd already rigged one. Or "fixed" it if you used her logic. All the more reason she'd do it again. But the school didn't use paper ballots for the Snow Princess vote. And Conor had confirmed that the online system wasn't hackable. Unless she'd figured out a way to do it? But Tessa was talking again.

"I thought that would be the end of it, but no. Almost every single club was the same thing. People passed over in favor of others who didn't deserve it. Cheaters. Liars. The *popular kids*."

"So you decided to take matters into your own hands."

She crossed her arms and raised an eyebrow at me. "As opposed to what you do?"

"The school paper?"

"Oh, don't play games with me, DJ. I know what you do. What you *all* do. Hatching plots. Righting wrongs."

The way she said it made me feel icky. It wasn't that she was being judgmental. It was that she wasn't. "I caught wind of what you guys were doing when you interrupted one of my operations."

"The foiled rocket boosting."

"I should thank you for that," she said. "My info was bad. It would have been a big mistake."

"All of what you're doing is a big mistake!" I countered. "We've been researching you, too, you know!"

"So you've seen all the people I've helped."

"And hurt! Yeah, maybe some of them had it coming, but most of them were innocent kids! Just because someone wins doesn't mean they didn't deserve it! I mean, you won the election! I voted for you! Is that why you hide your identity, even inside your little club? 'Cause you're the queen of the number two and you're literally the school president?"

Her eyes went dark. "I'll never be number one. Not really." She was thinking about Regina again, I could tell. But then her eyes lightened. "But I know you understand, considering what it is you do."

I shook my head. "We don't do the same thing."

"Don't we?"

"You work with criminals!"

She laughed. "And Mariposa's what? A Space Cadet?"

"It's all the same to you, I guess."

"Power is power," she said. "I don't like everyone I have to work with, but if I can control them, I can use their power for good."

"Right, because rigging an election is so good. Does Paige even know you're doing that?"

"No," said Tessa. "And she's not going to find out. The winter formal vote is the biggest popularity contest of them all. Someone like Paige could never win, even though she deserves it a million times more than Sienna."

"You're doing it because she's your friend. Do you not hear what you're saying? You're giving her special treatment because you're her friend! How is this different than any of the people you busted?"

"I know she deserves it most *because* she's my friend."

"It's not gonna work," I said. "Whatever you think you're going to do to rig it. If Conor can't do it, no one can. You'll get caught."

"Oh, I know," she said. "I talked to your friend. Malik?

Nice kid. Goes to school with my sister. He came over once to work on a school project with her, and we had an interesting conversation."

I knew it! Wrestling team? Give me a break.

"After the snowstorm knocked out the power and lost the nominations, I wanted to know if I could do that again on purpose," she continued. "Lose some votes for Paige's opponent. Malik said the same thing you did. I even had him double-check for me when he was here for wrestling practice. The system is airtight. No way to hack it without the school being alerted. Which is why it's not going to be rigged for Paige. It'll be rigged for Sienna. And when it gets found out—"

"They'll think she cheated for herself. She'll be disqualified." My eyes snapped up to meet hers. "Why are you telling me this? You know I'm going to stop you."

"Oh, you can't stop me," she said. "First of all, you don't have any proof. And second of all, it's already done. There was already an attempt to flood the system with bogus votes for Sienna an hour ago. They just haven't discovered it yet. But they will as soon as they check their email. I knew you'd get involved one way or another, DJ. That's why I needed a plan B and C. Keeping you busy is not an easy job. But once you locked on to Paige as your prime suspect, it took a lot of the heat off me, so thanks for that."

I'd given speeches like this. I'd been on the other side of this exchange so many times, lining up my verbal shots one after the other to back my opponent into a corner. But this time, I didn't feel like a hawk. I didn't even feel like a hawk having a bad day; I fully felt like prey. Like a mouse.

I tried to keep the shake out of my voice, but if she was as hawkeyed as me, I was sure she could tell it was a front.

"This still doesn't explain why you're telling me this," I said.

"Isn't it obvious?" she said. Her face went soft and welcoming. She didn't look like she wanted to take me down. She looked like genuine, friendly, kind Tessa again. "I told you, I respect what you do. I want you to work with me. Join the BPS. Or stay independent and we can be allies. We want the same things. We could do so much together, DJ."

I felt a wave of déjà vu wash over me. This was Lucky all over again. Except Lucky knew what he was about. Tessa thought she was the good guy here. She thought we were the same.

"Do I have a choice?" I asked.

She looked hurt. "I'm not going to force you, DJ. I don't force anyone to join the BPS. It's by invitation. I'm sure you know that."

"So, if I say no, you're just going to let me walk away with all this information?"

"I won't force you to join," she repeated, not actually answering my question. "But you don't have clean hands. I know why you're here. At the Fitz. Malik and I talked about more than just the election. We also talked about you. I know things about you. I have evidence. Things people here don't know about you. Things you don't want them to know. And I know who's in your crew here. Monty. Conor. *Audrey.*"

I kept still and emotionless, but she knew how to hit where it hurt. All the work I'd put into keeping everyone safe and undercover, and Tessa was rubbing it in my face.

"Not that I want anything to happen to them," she said. "The opposite, really. Brent, from choir? Do you know how badly he wanted a solo in the winter concert? Audrey's gotten them every year since we were little. He would have been an easy recruit, but I kept him out as a favor to you. So she wouldn't get caught up in any of this. Do you know what I could have done if I actually wanted to hurt you?"

I didn't care that Santiago could definitely beat the snot out of me. I took a step forward to get right in Tessa's face. "Is that a threat?"

"Does it sound like a threat?" she answered coolly.

We stood there, silently staring each other down for what felt like hours but was probably only seconds. I didn't want to give in, but I didn't have any leverage on her. Even if I felt confident enough to bluff her, I didn't know what that bluff would be. And she had so much dirt on me. On all of us. Would it be so bad to give in? Did we have a choice?

And then the auditorium door swung open.

"Oh, there you are, DJ!"

Audrey! It was Audrey! Santiago was too busy keeping me here to also keep others out. My brain ran through all the things I could say to try to signal something was wrong, but Tessa caught my eye and shook her head a fraction of a degree.

"Don't," she mouthed, the threat clear without her

having to say anything else. She tossed a glance at Santiago, who quickly dropped his bodyguard stance. Then she spun to meet Audrey, relaxed as if she hadn't just been threatening me.

"Someone said they saw you come this way," Audrey said as she made her way to the foot of the stage.

"We ran out of cups," Tessa said. "DJ said he knew where we could find some."

"Do you need help?" Audrey asked, looking directly at me.

YES. "No," I said, trying to stay just as casual as Tessa. "We're all good here. You should go back to the carnival."

"You sure? I don't mind."

I hesitated, took a quick glance at Tessa, then nodded. "Yeah. Don't worry. I don't need you."

"OK," she said cheerfully. "Find me after. We need to talk about newspaper stuff. Bye, Tessa. Bye, Santiago."

"See ya, Audrey," she said as my last hope retreated out of the room.

Tessa turned her attention back to me. "Good. I knew you'd do the right thing."

"Lying to my friend?"

"Keeping her out of it," Tessa countered. "I know

you do it. I know there's a reason that as far as anyone in the know knows, DJ works with Monty and Conor. Not everyone knows about her. You protect her."

"She doesn't need protecting."

She smiled at me indulgently. Like I was a kid saying I didn't take any cake while my face was smeared with chocolate. "Come on, DJ. You don't believe that."

I closed my eyes. I thought about Audrey saving my and Conor's butts behind the Starcade the first time we were together as a group by bursting into fake tears. I thought about her annoyance in the hallway when she'd tried to give me that lollipop. I thought about our lunch . . . date? Whatever that had been.

My eyes snapped open. I wasn't sure how I was going to deal with Tessa, but I was sure about Audrey.

"Yes, I do," I said, voice perfectly even for the first time since this conversation started. "She can stand on her own, and so can Paige. Do you think she'd be happy to know what you're doing on her behalf?"

There was a twitch in her expression again, but it wasn't the same as before. That had been annoyance. Anger. Triggered by her sister. What was this?

"She'd understand." A lie.

"Then why don't you tell her?"

"Because she doesn't need to know." Another lie. And that twitch again. A twinge of . . . guilt?

"You wouldn't say that if you didn't think you were doing something wrong."

"You don't know what I'd say."

"Don't I?" Yeah, definitely guilt. Maybe I didn't have anything concrete to use as leverage, but that didn't mean I couldn't hit her where it hurt. I didn't move from where I was standing, but I somehow felt less cornered. "You're the one who keeps saying we're the same. Maybe I keep Audrey out of the thick of things sometimes and that's wrong, but I always tell her what we're doing."

Bam. A hit. I could see it in her eyes.

"I don't lie to my team."

Hit.

"I don't lie to my friends."

Hit.

"If you think you're doing right, you should have no problem telling Paige."

"Telling me what?" said a voice from behind the curtains.

Any composure Tessa had retained melted away as she jumped high enough to get on-the-spot drafted to the basketball team. The curtains behind us parted, revealing Mariposa, Monty, Conor, Audrey, and a very disoriented-looking Paige.

Tessa looked shocked, truly shocked for the first time since she'd started talking. It wasn't just flashes. She was fully knocked out of boss mode. The hawk look was gone from her eyes. She looked more like a deer in headlights.

"Paige!" she said, her voice jumping half an octave. "What are you doing here?" She glanced at me, and I shrugged. She had my phone. I couldn't text anyone. And she'd heard my conversation with Audrey. I hadn't asked for help.

"They said you had something to say to me," Paige said, looking at Audrey and Mariposa and then back at me. "They brought me here. Were you just talking about me?"

"What? Of course not."

"Oh, come on," Conor said. "Don't give us that. We totally heard you guys say her name."

"Oh, well, yeah, 'cause we were talking about winter formal stuff, right, DJ?"

She turned to me and gave me a look with a glint that said, *Remember what I know.*

I pulled a pen out of my pocket. "Do you know what this is?" I asked. "Spy pen. From Conor's kit. You said you and Paige used to play around with invisible-ink pens, so maybe you've heard of these, too. It has a recorder. I've been recording this whole time."

Tessa might have had a good front, but you're only as good as your team, and in that moment, the other member of her team? Santiago?

He said, "Wait, what? You were recording?" Then he covered his mouth with his hands.

She shot him a withering look and then turned back to Paige, who looked even more confused.

"What's going on, Tess?"

"You better tell her," I said, thumb hovering over the pen. "Tell her or I will. Or, actually, I'll just press this button, and she'll hear it herself."

"Hear what?"

Tessa threw her hands up. "Paige, it's not what it's gonna sound like, I promise. I did it for you, for everyone."

"Did what?"

"Rigged the Snow Princess vote, for starters," said Audrey.

I turned to Paige. "She said you couldn't have won without her."

"And I guess that means she did all the other BPS stuff, too," said Monty. "Stealing Jade's tuba before her band test."

"Leaving Hailey that nasty note before her solo," Audrey added.

"Let's not forget freaking out Dominic before the spelling bee and losing me one thousand tickets," said Conor.

Paige looked more and more concerned as we spoke. "You did all that?" she said.

"No! Paige, of course not!"

I twitched my thumb over the top of the pen, and she flinched.

"OK, I might have organized some stuff, but I didn't do it personally! It was all the BPS."

"What's the BPS?"

"Paige, we can just get out of here. W-we don't have to listen to this."

"What's the BPS?" she demanded again. It was the loudest I've ever heard Paige speak.

"It doesn't matter." And that was the quietest I've ever heard Tessa speak.

"It does! Why would you do all that? The spelling bee? And the dance? Why—?"

"Because you weren't gonna win if I didn't, Paige! And you deserved to win! Not Sienna! It's not fair!"

When she'd been talking to me before, she'd sounded like a crusader. Like a freedom fighter. Like a rebel with a cause. But now? She sounded like a kid who didn't get the toy they wanted for Christmas. And I think that's what Paige heard, too, because she took a step, crossing downstage toward Tessa as she spoke. Voice getting louder with each step.

"Do you think I care about winning? Tessa, I've never cared about any of that! It's always you! You cared about being president. I just ran with you 'cause you wanted to. You're the one who wanted to do this whole carnival. You're the one who nominated me! I didn't even want to do it. You said it would be fun!"

"It will be!" Tessa said, her voice strained. She rushed to close the last few feet between them and grabbed Paige's hands. "It'll be fun when you win and they crown you and everyone stops calling you Tractor Tran and—"

"I don't care!" Paige yelled, snatching away her hands. "I don't care what people call me! Why do you?"

"B-because we're friends."

Paige looked down. Then she looked up at Tessa, eyes cold and hard. "Not anymore." And she took off backstage.

"Paige!" Tessa said, running after her.

I shot a glance at Monty, who blocked her path.

"Audrey," I said.

"On it." She ducked under Monty's arm and went after Paige.

I looked over at Tessa, who didn't even look like a deer anymore. She looked like a kid whose best friend had just said she wanted nothing to do with her. No fight. No flight. Nothing. It almost felt bad hitting her any harder, but we had to end this. Permanently.

"Audrey will talk to her," I said. "I don't know what she's going to say exactly, but like I said before, I trust her." Tessa looked away from me, but she couldn't hide the expression on her face now. Shame.

"Oh, and just so you know, this isn't a recording pen." I clicked the top a few times. "Just a ballpoint. But you just confessed to everything again, so I'm hoping—"

I glanced over at Conor, who held up his phone with a grin. "Mariposa's still rigged up for sound. I got it all!" He pressed a button, and Tessa's voice echoed in the empty auditorium, *"Because you weren't gonna win if I didn't, Paige!"*

"Perfect."

At this point, Santiago bolted for the front door.

"Monty," I said, and he took off after him. I didn't bother looking up to see if he caught him. It was Monty.

Instead, I squared up against Tessa and held out a hand. She looked confused for a second before a dim recognition lit in her eyes and she handed my phone back to me.

I slid it into my back pocket and caught her eyes so she couldn't look away. "All right, Tessa. Let's talk."

CHAPTER TWENTY-TWO
VANISHING ACT

Like I said before, there was one big difference between Lucky and Tessa. She thought she was doing the right thing. Once her furious *former* friend threw that into question, she was a completely different person.

While Audrey handled Paige, I tied up loose ends with Tessa, and she answered questions with no fight. Yes, she was the ringleader. Yes, she'd rigged the election. Yes, she'd done it without Paige's knowledge.

"You have to turn yourself in," I said. "If you don't—"

"I'll do it," she said, staring blankly ahead. "I'll do it today. I . . ." She looked up at me. "She's never going to talk to me again, is she?"

I hesitated. "I don't know. She's your friend."

Tessa made a sound that was almost a laugh but not quite. "Is she?" She looked like she was thinking. Then she said, "I don't know if she'll talk to me later, but she for sure won't talk to me now. Can you tell her . . . can you tell her that I'm going to confess? To everything. And . . . and that I'm sorry. I'm really, really sorry."

"I can do that," I said. "But you need to go talk to the principal now. About the election. You can deal with the BPS stuff later, but that needs to be fixed now."

She quirked a smile, an actual one this time. A shadow of her full Disney Channel smile, but real. "I never thought I'd end up in the principal's office. Or that he'd have red hair when it happened." She sighed. "OK. I'm ready."

I looked up at Monty. "Go with her. Make sure she actually does it."

"You don't trust me?"

"Honestly? I do." And I did. I didn't think Tessa was a bad person. She'd let her personal issues blow up into a huge mess that had hurt a lot of people—some innocent, some not—but now that she'd been snapped back to reality, I did trust her. But she still had to face the music, and I had to make sure that happened.

Monty looked at Santiago, who he was still holding

by the collar, and back at me. "What do I do with him?" he asked.

Mariposa stepped forward. "Don't worry. I've got him. Santiago, let's go backstage. You and me are gonna have a little chat." And Santiago somehow went even paler.

Tessa gave me one last look and then turned to go, Monty following behind her.

As she did, there was a ping on my phone. Audrey.

Talked to Paige. Got her to hold off on talking for now. We can control the situation.

I smiled and texted her back. *Awesome. And thank you for saving my butt in there. I was hoping you'd get my signal.*

Audrey: *:) How could I miss it? I seem to remember a certain someone telling me on a lunch date that he never wanted me to feel like he didn't "need me."*

I was glad the job was over, because poker face aside, nothing could have stopped me from smiling like an idiot at that.

Before I could send another text, Conor tackled me from behind. "Dude!"

"I know."

"That was—!"

"I know!" Now that I was out of the immediate danger zone, it was beginning to hit me how much had just happened in such a short amount of time. We'd been in the middle of a completely different, also super-risky, plan before I'd ended up cornered by the head of the criminal secret society we were chasing.

"That was epic!" Conor crowed.

Sure, if *epic* was a synonym for "the most nerve-racking thing I'd ever done."

"Audrey came running out of nowhere like, 'DJ is in trouble!' We literally figured out the whole thing on the fly. We were booking it. Monty was running with Mariposa on his shoulders 'cause she couldn't keep up. No joke. It was the wildest thing I've seen in my life! I wish I'd taken a picture. What were you gonna do if Audrey didn't figure out what was going on?"

I put a hand on his shoulder. "Conor, I'm gonna be real with you. I don't know. Tessa has so much dirt on us. Like, even from before the Fitz. It sounds like Malik told her everything."

"Dang, for real?"

"Yeah, but I think we're safe. I don't think she's gonna tell. And . . . I don't know what I would have done, but I know we would have figured it out. Together."

"Yeah, man, always." He put out a fist, and I tapped it with mine.

"Hey, you down for a Starcade run after the bell rings? I think we deserve a break."

"You know it," Conor said. "But lemme grab some doughnuts from the carnival first. I know Tessa's a bad guy and everything, but those doughnuts are amazing."

I let him go and decided to track down Mariposa. I wasn't Santiago's biggest fan right now, but I didn't want her going overboard, either.

I poked my head out of the backstage and saw Mariposa leaning against the wall, one shoe pressed flat against it like she was waiting for me. Santiago was nowhere to be seen. I squinted at her.

"Don't give me that look," she said. "He's fine. He also isn't going to say anything to tip off the other BPS members that we're onto them. You're welcome."

I thought about prying deeper but decided against it. I'd uncovered more than enough already today.

"I'll have to report back to Lucky," Mariposa said. "He'll probably want to talk to you, too."

"Fair enough," I said. I didn't like the idea of him thinking he could just summon me whenever, but there was no reason to be difficult, and honestly, I kinda wanted to talk to him, too, to get a gauge of where we stood.

"I'm going to debrief him tonight, and then I'll be in touch when he wants to meet."

I smiled slightly. "I don't see why I can't just talk to you. Seems like you've been running things just fine while Lucky's been away. Weren't you tempted by her offer at all?"

She scoffed. "Which of us had a target on our back? Me or Lucky? Yeah, I think I'm fine where I am, thanks." Then she hesitated and said, "I heard you're having a team thing at the Starcade."

"Yeah. How—"

"The acoustics in here are very good, and you and Conor are very loud. Don't worry, I'm not going. I know you all don't want me at your good-guy celebration party."

"Monty might."

She glared at me, but her heart wasn't in it.

"He's like a teddy bear," I said. "You're allowed to like

him without ruining your whole tough-girl thing. I won't snitch on you to Lucky."

"I don't care about Monty."

"Tyler beaned him with a baseball at the carnival today."

The heat on her glare turned up to blazing. "He did *what*? Oh, he is getting rocket boosted first thing on Monday."

I raised my eyebrow at her.

"Fine. The kid grows on you."

"He's weirdly friendly, right?"

"It's bizarre," she admitted before shaking her head. "Anyway, here."

She handed over four coupons. They were for the Starcade. Pizza and token tickets. The kind you got as a reward for good grades or a good deed. I thought about asking whether they were forged or swiped but decided against it. Professional courtesy, and besides, why would she tell me?

I slipped them into my pocket. "Thanks. And leave Tyler alone. Monty walked into the ball because I told him to. If you're gonna be mad at anyone for that, it should be me."

She scanned me up and down like she was considering

it before giving a little nod. "Fine, but he's on thin ice." It seemed like she was getting ready to go, but then she said, "One more thing. Do you know who it was who tipped you off? The person who put the pencil in your locker in the first place?"

I shook my head. "No. Wasn't really the most important thing, and then everything moved so quickly. I didn't really have the chance to figure it out. Why? Do you have an idea?"

"No, I just thought it would be nice to know if there was someone on my side prone to snitching. And I still have to figure out how Conor's cheats were leaked to Ambrose so I can take care of that."

"Oh." Right, this was still Mariposa. We'd worked together for this, but she was still playing her side and I was playing mine. "Well, I guess we go back to being . . . whatever we were before now, huh?"

"If you're asking if I'll still have you rocket boosted if you get in our way, the answer is: in a heartbeat."

I raised an eyebrow. "Even Monty?"

"Shut up." She started walking away, and as she did she said without turning around, "And go to the dance with Audrey, you dummy. Geez."

For once, I was glad for one of Mariposa's dramatic exits, because even though I couldn't actually turn red, I knew it was obvious that I was blushing.

A little bit later, the whole gang was munching on pizza and sitting in the most isolated booth in the Starcade. Conor spun the shard of pencil that had started it all on the table like a top.

"I can't believe it. All this over half a pencil."

Audrey picked it up from the table and held it up to her eyes. "I know. I honestly would have just thrown it away. Even with the note."

Monty reached for it, and Audrey handed it over. He didn't say anything for a second and then he said, "It's sad."

"Uh, what?" said Conor. "What are you talking about, dude, it's awesome! We did it!"

"Not us," he said. "Paige and Tessa. They're such good friends. Or were, at least. Do you think they're gonna be friends again?"

It was like hearing an echo in someone else's voice. Tessa had asked me the same question barely an hour ago. That friendship had been real. The look in her eyes when she was telling that farm story. Or when she was talking about them having sleepovers and doing Halloween costumes together and writing messages to each other in . . . in . . .

"Invisible ink," I whispered.

"What?" said Monty.

"Invisible ink!" I repeated, grabbing my cup of tokens and rushing across the Starcade. I slowed down slightly as I passed the prize counter just to make sure the thing that I wanted was still an option. Five hundred tickets? No problem.

By the time the rest of the gang caught up with me, I was already dropping a token into Rowdy Roundup.

"DJ, what's up?" said Conor. "I know you didn't come here to play games."

"I need the tickets," I said. I still remembered the patterns needed for a perfect game. One jackpot would be enough.

"What does—"

"Shh," said Audrey. "Let him concentrate."

Pigs, sheep, and cows came down the screen, and I matched them as quickly as I could. There wasn't actually a rush, but it felt urgent somehow. I needed to know. With the last animal in place, the jackpot alarm went off and tickets began to scroll out of the machine.

"Invisible ink," I said again, trying to explain now that I wasn't caught up in the game. "Tessa mentioned she and Paige used to play with invisible-ink pens when they were younger and write messages to each other."

"So?" said Conor. "So did we."

"Yeah, I know," I said, ripping the tickets off and hurrying to the counter machine. "And how do they work?"

"You write the message and then there's a little light on the pen cap and you squeeze it and—oh!"

"Exactly!"

Before Audrey or Monty could ask, I turned to them. "When Conor and I met with Royce in the boys' bathroom, he checked our pencils. Well, not him, one of his guys. And he checked it with a little light, and I didn't get why at the time but—"

The ticket machine stopped counting—they really were a lot faster than the old ones—and I slammed the print button as fast as I could. As soon as the receipt spat out, I raced over to the prize counter.

"One invisible-ink pen, please!"

The employee grabbed one from below the counter and handed it to me. "You still have five hundred tickets—"

"Keep the change!"

I ran back over to the group. "Who has the pencil?"

Monty produced it as I ripped the pen out of its packaging and pulled the UV light cap off. I took a breath, then shone the light on the pencil.

At first there was nothing. And then, as I turned the pencil around, there was a mark. And then a name. Jude.

"Oh!" said Conor. "They were marked with invisible ink."

"Oh no," said Monty. "I didn't know that when I made my fake. I'm really sorry."

"It worked, though," Conor pointed out. "We didn't get caught."

"But Jude had the light," I said. "He would have seen that your pencil didn't have a name on it and mine had his name on it. But he didn't react, and he didn't snitch on us. And there's only one reason for that." I closed my hand around the pencil shard. "Guys, I think we found our loose end."

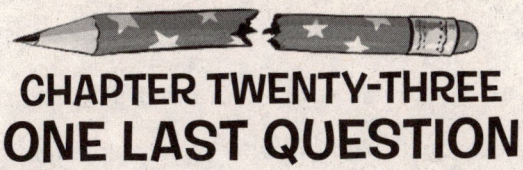

CHAPTER TWENTY-THREE
ONE LAST QUESTION

I was never eager to go back on campus once I'd left it, but for this I'd make an exception. Some TKs—like Mariposa—got to school early and some—like Jude—stayed late. Later than kids in clubs. Late enough to pick up pencils from a certain locker without prying eyes spotting them.

I knew where his mom's classroom was, and when I checked, she wasn't in there—but he was, sitting in her swivel chair, doing homework. Looked like math.

"Hey, Jude," I said casually. He looked up and dropped his pencil when he saw it was me.

I rushed forward. "Oh, lemme get that." I bent to pick it up, then I stopped and fished the broken pencil out of my pocket. "Or maybe you want this back instead."

He was quiet for a second. And then he said, "David said you were good."

Oh. He was a referral from David. That made sense. "I'm sure he also said I was trustworthy. Why didn't you just come to me? This would have been a lot faster if we didn't have to play connect the dots about what was even happening."

"You don't know her."

"Oh, I think we do," I said. "But you're right. That does answer the question. She's powerful. And well-connected. I can see why you'd be nervous to talk."

I stood there, eyes on him, not trying to stare him down but letting him know I wasn't planning on leaving without answers. He was silent. All I could hear was the hum of the fluorescent lights and the ticking from the wall clock. They didn't bother me. I had time.

After a few seconds he spoke.

"I was one of the first in," he said. "And it wasn't even over a club. My math teacher—Mr. Sherman—always gives a Snickers bar to the kid who scores highest on their math test. I'm the best student in that class—my mom is literally a math teacher! But Brandon cheats. He gets the questions from his friend in the first-period class." He gave a sad little laugh. "Isn't that dumb? To get that upset over a Snickers bar?"

"Sometimes it's more about the principle," I said, thinking about Tessa.

He seemed to roll that around in his head. Then: "I mentioned it to Tessa when she interviewed me during Chess Club. She said she could help. And she did. She got tests planted in his locker. He got suspended for a week. But then I had to keep doing stuff for her. I have connections because of my mom. I was too useful for her to let go. And I'd already taken her help. She said that if I didn't help her, the whole thing would get found out and I'd get in trouble, too. I didn't know what to do."

He looked away from me again, and when he looked up, his eyes were glossy, like he might cry. "Am I going to get in trouble?" His voice sounded so small.

"Not from Tessa," I said, trying to sound reassuring. "And not from me. There are still things that need to be sorted out, but if your story is true, you should be fine. Just sit tight; we'll talk later." I turned to go and then stopped. "Oh, and when you see David? Tell him he owes me so many lollipops."

The gang was waiting for me outside. Their heads snapped to attention as soon as the door opened.

"Well?" said Conor.

"Loose end tied," I said. "We still have cleanup to do, but our mystery is officially solved."

I expected some fist pumps, high fives, at least some smiles, but instead, Conor and Monty shot Audrey a look. It was the same look I used to share with Conor when we were getting into trouble.

"What?" I said.

Monty nudged Audrey forward.

"Don't worry," Conor said in a stage whisper. "If he says no, we'll beat him up."

She smiled at him and then turned to me.

"Am I getting beat up?" I asked.

"I hope not," she said teasingly.

"What were you talking about?"

She looked back at the guys and then at me. "Well, I was just thinking. It would be kind of a shame for us to save the winter formal and then not even get to go, you know? No one besides Mariposa and Tessa and Paige are going to know what we did. We're not gonna get a round of applause. The least we can do is go. And besides, what if something else happens? Who else could stop it?"

"You know?" I said. "You make an excellent point."

"Yeah?"

"Yeah. I mean, if you're asking what I think you're asking."

"I'm asking you to the winter formal," Audrey said while Conor and Monty said, at the same time, "She's asking you to the winter formal."

"At a certain point, a girl just has to take matters into her own hands. We don't have to be super flashy about it if you don't want, and the guys will be there, too, so we'll have cover, and if we need to do the reporter thing, then—"

"Audrey," I said, cutting her off.

"Yeah?"

"I'd love to go to the winter formal with you."

And the high fives I got for that were better than for any job.

Lucky was back at school the next day. When I opened my locker before class on Friday, two things fell out: four dance tickets stapled together and a summons.

I rolled into the library during third period to find Lucky in his usual spot for the first time in almost a month. His crutches were laid out on the seat next to him. It seemed like he wasn't fully healed yet, but he looked no less intimidating. In the seat next to him was Mariposa, looking unfriendly as ever. Things were officially back to normal. But she *had* left us the tickets. Did that mean anything? Did Lucky know?

Lucky gestured for me to take a seat.

"DJ," he said, sounding as cordial as someone like him could. "I hear you and Mariposa got into a lot of trouble while I was away."

"You could say that," I answered, sitting down across from him.

"'You could say that'?" He barked out an incredulous laugh and swatted Mariposa on the side. "You hear this? You two sniff out an entire conspiracy happening under our noses and take out the ringleader and he says, 'You could say that.' Unbelievable. I swear, every time we talk I'm just thinking, why doesn't this kid work for me?" He must have seen me shift into defense mode because he raised a hand. "Relax, DJ. This isn't a recruitment meeting. Though you and your boys are welcome to join the team anytime."

Boys? Did he still not know about—? I slid my eyes over to Mariposa. She didn't move an inch. Huh.

"We just wanted to let you know, as a courtesy, that Tessa is being dealt with by the authorities. It hasn't hit the news yet, but she's been suspended. Impeached. She'll have to go to mandatory counseling. Of course, she's getting off easier than I'd like."

I thought about Tessa having to tell her parents what she'd done, knowing her sister would find out, her best friend not answering any of her texts.

"You call that easy?"

"Compared to what I'd do to her? That's a trip to Disney World."

I wasn't scared of Lucky, but the way he said that made me remember why other kids were.

"I'll be handling all the cleanup related to my side of the game," he continued. "You don't try to cross me without repercussions. Mariposa's going to make sure everything on our end is wrapped up nice and neat, and then?" He counted off with his fingers. "Three, two, one, blastoff."

I shuddered internally. What Lucky did to other criminals wasn't really any of my business, and Lucky's iron fist did keep things contained in a way. But it was still very not fun to think about. It looked like Pluto was going to have some new inhabitants soon enough.

"So don't be doing any vigilante justice on my guys the way you do, OK?" he said. "I have it handled. And hey? Enjoy the dance on me. I'm not going—broken leg and all—but that doesn't mean you shouldn't have fun. Consider it payment for the assistance. I always pay my debts, after all. Maybe you'll realize I'm not such a bad guy and reconsider my offer. I even had Mariposa get two extra tickets so your bodyguard and thief friend can go, too. See? No hard feelings."

This time when I glanced over at her, Mariposa was nonchalantly inspecting her nails.

"Lucky," I said, "I promise, if I ever decide I'm more interested in joining huge criminal conspiracies than taking them down, you'll be the first person I call."

He raised one eyebrow slightly. "You know, a person could interpret that as a threat."

"A threat? From me?" I scoffed. "Come on, Lucky. You know I'm too busy for that. I have a dance to get ready for."

EPILOGUE: LIKE NOBODY'S WATCHING

Whatever else you could say about Tessa, that girl knew how to plan a party.

The gym was completely transformed. Twinkle lights made the paper snowflakes hung from the ceiling seem to shimmer. An avalanche of white and ice-blue balloons covered the floor, walls, and fake trees that were placed around the space. I almost felt like Queen Elsa was gonna bust in and start singing "Let It Go."

I popped a snowball doughnut hole into my mouth, careful not to get powdered sugar on my black suit. My mom had bought me the suit six months ago for the wedding of some uncle I'd never met in my life. I hadn't been thrilled at the time, but you better believe I was happy to see it in my closet when I was getting dressed for the dance.

Audrey also hadn't known that we were going to the dance until the last minute, but the way she was dressed, you'd never be able to tell. Her dress was pale blue and glittery with ruffles at the bottom and poofy, princessy sleeves.

When she'd opened her front door and I saw the dress for the first time, she'd held up her hands and said, "If it's too flashy I have a plan B but—"

"Don't change," I'd said. "You look great. Uh, sorry I don't match."

But she'd pulled a strip of matching blue fabric from behind her back and carefully tucked it into my front pocket, patting it twice once she was done.

"There," she'd said with a satisfied smile. "Now you do."

Back in the gym, I got a napkin to wipe the sugar off my hands and then adjusted my pocket square. Audrey had dipped away for a second to take pictures with her choir friends, so I was scanning the room. It was weird to see certain people here and all dressed up, knowing what we knew. Kennedy, in a purple gown, talking to one of the mathletes. Duncan in a tux T-shirt with his band bros. Ambrose still in his stupid dress shirt and tie. Just enjoying the dance like nothing had happened. All while Tessa and Paige were noticeably absent. They might have been lower-level members of the organization, but they'd willingly hurt people to get positions they still had. Someone had to do something about it.

But that could wait, because Audrey was coming back with two cans of soda.

"Thanks," I said, taking the one she offered me and popping the tab. "And I know I said it already, but you look great."

"You've actually said it *six* times already. But if you want to keep going, I'm not gonna stop you." She giggled and spun around so that her dress flared out. "Did I mention it was a Halloween costume? The year before we met, I was Glinda from *Wicked*. My mom just helped me get rid of some of the ruffles, and I left the wand and tiara at home. We're friends now, but I think Sienna would be pretty mad if I showed up in a tiara on her big day. It would be like wearing white to someone else's wedding. Scandalous!"

"Yeah, well, even without the tiara, you're for sure princess material, and Sienna is just gonna have to deal with that."

She blushed deeply without trying to hide it and elbowed me in the side. "Aww, DJ. I thought sweet-talking was my job."

I elbowed her back. "Just telling the truth. Hey, do you see Conor? I haven't seen him in a hot second, which makes me nervous."

She waved a hand. "Don't worry about him. There's a group of kids in the boys' bathroom playing soda roulette with shaken-up soda cans, and Conor decided to start a betting pool."

I rolled my eyes. "If he put half as much energy into his homework as he did on this stuff, he'd be a straight A student."

"Yeah, but then he wouldn't be Conor. And don't worry, Monty is with him."

That did make me feel a little better. I was going to ask to see the pictures she'd taken with her friends when Jenna Tucker walked by, her dress as colorful as the pottery she'd had destroyed so she could win the competition.

"You're still thinking about it, aren't you?" Audrey asked.

"Trying not to," I said. "At least for tonight. I feel like we need to do something but . . . you don't think I'm like Tessa, do you? Like, I want to make things better, but not like her. I know we break the rules sometimes, but—"

She stopped me with a finger to my lips.

"DJ," she said firmly. "If you ever decide to go on a power trip and end up totally off the rails, Conor, Monty, and I will bonk you on the head until you stop. You're not alone like she was. But, either way, it's not gonna be an issue. You're a good person, DJ. And we're gonna figure out what to do about the BPS. Together."

She moved her finger, and my lips burned where she'd touched me. Actually, all of me was burning up, even though the room looked so snowy.

The music suddenly switched. A slow song. The energy in the room shifted. This wasn't, like, jump-up-and-down-with-your-buds music. This was slow-dance music. The dance floor began to separate like oil and water—girls on one side, boys on the other—as kids shuffled away to get food or go to the bathroom or just stand on the sidelines.

Middle school dances aren't that great, I'd said to Conor a few weeks ago. *Everyone just stands around awkwardly and doesn't dance.* My prophecy was coming true.

"This is a really pretty song," Audrey said, sipping her soda. She was just staring into space, not really paying attention.

I looked at the almost-empty dance floor. I looked at Audrey. I slammed the rest of my soda.

"Wanna dance?"

She almost dropped her soda. "What?"

"We should go dance," I repeated. "If you want to."

"I—I do, but—" She looked around. "There's, like, no one out there. People will see us for sure. Like, *everyone* will see us."

"Good," I said. "Let them see. You're a super-good dancer." I held out my hand.

She hesitated. "Are you sure? You aren't worried? I thought you wanted baby steps. It's safer your way."

I shrugged. "Yeah, but it's better your way. Plus, we have each other's backs." Out of the corner of my eye, I spotted Conor dipping into the room to grab some more soda cans. He caught my eyes and flashed me a thumbs-up. "All of us."

She grinned. "All right, then." And she took my hand as we walked onto the dance floor.

ACKNOWLEDGMENTS

As always, huge thank yous to my agent Emily who helped shepherd this novel from idea to full-fledged sequel and my editor Anna, who was at the ready with helpful suggestions on where I needed to add more "helicopter chases."

Thanks to my always supportive beta readers Sharon, Melanie, and Camille for helping me make sure I didn't lose the thread of my fictional conspiracy.

Shout out to my MFA classmates who never ratted me out for editing this book during class time: Rachel, Andi, Hal, Erin, Elizabeth, Jade, and Tom.

Thanks to my mom and dad who frequently called and asked me, "Is the new book done yet?"

And last but not least, thanks to my brother Michael, for always keeping me inspired when it comes to lovable troublemakers.

Read on for a sneak peek of *High Score*!

I walked back to class, numb.

Even though I had understood every word Lucky had said to me, they didn't really register. It was like when you read a textbook about some historical event that happened two hundred years ago and you know it happened and you know it's important but you don't feel connected to it at all.

Conor had tried to scam Lucky, and in less than twenty-four hours, he was getting rocket boosted. Right, and the Declaration of Independence was signed in 1776. How long till lunch?

But then it was lunchtime, and when I saw Conor waiting for me at the entrance of the cafeteria, looking sheepish, everything hit me at once.

Conor had tried to scam Lucky, and in less than twenty-four hours, he was getting rocket boosted.

"There you are," he said, sounding relieved. "I—"

Before he could say another word, I hit him on the arm, as hard as I could.

"OW! The heck, man?"

"I told you one thing," I hissed at him. "One thing: Don't mess with Lucky. And what do you immediately do?"

"Look, it's not as bad as it—wait. How do you know what happened? I didn't tell you yet."

"HOW DO I—?" I realized we were still standing right where everyone was coming in and I was starting to yell, so I pulled Conor into a corner and tried again, more softly. "How do I know? Because Lucky got Mariposa to pull me from class so we could 'chat.' About *you*."

He grinned. "Oh, great. So you already sorted it out."

"Sorted it—how do you expect me to sort it out?"

"What type of question is that? You're DJ! You have connections! You sit down, have a chat, and you walk out, problem solved!"

"*Had*. I *had* connections at Grover. I'm no one here! I can't just snap my fingers and it's all good!"

He shrugged. "OK, so you make one of your plans and—"

"GAH! How many times do I have to tell you? I'm done with plans. I'm done with tricks. I'm done with bailing you out of trouble because you can't just cool it for *one week*."

He flinched a little at that before crossing his arms and taking a step back. "What? You're so mad at me that you're gonna keep pretending even when I'm in trouble?"

"You're only in trouble because you didn't listen to me! You *never* listen to me and then everything goes too far and then I'm changing schools because I feel so guilty that I can't walk through the front doors without wanting to puke!" I could feel my voice rising, but I didn't care. I was too upset. And based on the way his eyes were narrowed, he was just as upset.

HEISTS, HIJINKS, AND HELPING OUT THE UNDERDOGS

My name's Darius James—but everyone calls me DJ. At my old school, I was the go-to guy for all kinds of tricky problems that needed creative solutions. But at my new school, Ella Fitzgerald Middle, I'm just trying to blend in. Until someone needs my help, anyway.

PRAISE FOR *HIGH SCORE*:

★ "A fast-paced adventure packed with cunning twists."
—*Publishers Weekly*, starred review

★ "A gleeful middle-school spin on *Ocean's Eleven*."
—*Booklist*, starred review

"An exciting and entertaining heist story."
—*Kirkus Reviews*